FOUND in the SCARS

FOUND in the SCARS

Michelle Janene

STRONG TOWER
PRESS

Sacramento, CA

Strong Tower Press, Sacramento, CA
strongtowerpress.com

Scriptures are taken from *English Standard Version Bible*. London: Crossway, 2010. Print. All rights reserved.

Cover Art by: Whetstone Designs
Images: Hands: Jacob Lund / Scar: kvdkz / Fence: volgariver purchased from Adobe Stock
Cover Fonts: Didot and Mongoose

ISBN-978-1-942320-36-4

Chapter 1

Muscles screamed and hands stung as Jeff wrestled with the quarter-inch-thick full sheet of plywood. The unwieldy lumber wouldn't slide in the bed of his pickup. Sweat ran in streams down his back, but he refused—as always—to remove his hoodie while in public. He could cool off at home. But only if he could ever get this da—

The board floated and quickly slid into the bed. Jeff stared at it, dumbfounded.

"Ready for the next one?"

Jeff jumped at the feminine voice. A woman held one side of the next sheet of plywood. She wore short jeans that stopped below her knees and a brightly colored flowing blouse. The blistering Sacramento sun lit streaks of gold in her wheat-colored hair.

Jeff remained hidden inside his hood, and peeked at her from the shadows within. "You don't need to help. I can—"

"Oh, come on." Her gentle coaxing and bright smile reached into his darkness. It revealed laugh lines around her mouth and eyes, telling him she smiled often. She might have been close to his age. He'd forgotten what smiling felt like, however. "It will be far easier with a little help." She wiggled her side of the next slab of wood. "It'll only take us a minute."

He doubted her estimation of their capabilities. He'd purchased enough to rebuild his shed blown down in a late spring storm. "You'll get splinters." When was the last time he'd talked to anyone other than his clients over the phone? Here this ray of light smiled on him and offered to assist him. He needed so much help. His loneliness overwhelmed him.

"Not if we do it right. Come on." It appeared again. Her radiant smile. How could one simple turn of the lips wrap him in a hug? When had someone last touched him? He tugged his hood a little lower over his face.

Jeff bent and retrieved his side of the next sheet, careful to remain inside his shroud. The plywood lifted with ease. Her hidden strength belied her feminine frame. She sidestepped toward the truck, and carried the large piece over the wheel well. He dropped his side too as she walked back to the full flatbed cart. The end of the sheet they'd placed inside sat dangling off the tailgate, and she gave it a shove with her hip.

"Two down, only a few more to go." She already had the next sheet in hand. Jeff struggled to keep up with her.

As his truck bed filled, he gasped for breath in the growing heat. He noted the thin sheen of perspiration above her lip.

When they finished, Jeff thought about racing back into the store and buying another load to keep her here. Years of lonely misery had addled his brain. But his desperation made him want to spend a couple of more minutes with her.

She brushed her hands free of any sawdust. "I hope you have help to unload this wherever you're going." She picked up her purse near the back wheel of an SUV parked two spots away. "Have a great day."

"Thank you." Jeff had followed her like a lost puppy, and extended his right, gloved hand. He usually shook with his left—if he touched anyone at all. "I would have been here for hours without your help. I don't know how to repay you."

Her grip was strong yet gentle as it nestled inside of his. "Nothing to thank. We can all use an extra pair of hands now and then." Her voice was neither high nor low. It slid through her perfect rosy lips with the same carefree manner as she'd helped him.

"Will you need any help loading your items?" What compelled him to push this hard? Keep your head down, get away from people—especially beautiful, smiling ones—stay hidden. He'd lived like this for the last two decades. Alone. But now, fifty-one years old, he couldn't bear it another moment.

She pulled a couple of items out of her pocket with her free hand. "Nah, all I need is to find new replacements for these thingies and one of the bar things that hooks to the bulb-floating thing in the toilet. Little stuff." She still gripped his hand.

And *he* hadn't pulled away.

An errant gust of wind from a passing delivery truck snatched his hood back over his shoulders. He jerked. Exposed. His hideous face unmasked for her to recoil from. The sweat caking his body froze, along with his heart.

Her smile never faded. Her gaze never left his. She saw it, didn't she? The wretched scar covering the right side of his face. Smooth blotchy pink and white skin; how could she miss it? Still she held his hand, her smile hugged him tight.

Jeff scrambled to retrieve and replace the hood. "Sorry," he muttered, and cowered under his shroud once more.

She shrugged. "We all have scars." No disgust tainted her voice. No condemnation. But then she didn't know how he'd come by his. She'd never speak to him if she knew the truth. Yet for now, she still hadn't turned away—or released his hand.

"May I help you find your emitters, fogger on barbs, and a float arm?"

"Barbs on foggers … arms?" She chuckled. "No wonder I can't find anything in this store. Who came up with these names?"

"Probably a man."

She laughed and finally released her grasp. "It's a conspiracy, right? All the men got together and made home improvement and car repair as confusing and complicated as possible. In middle school when they separate us for PE, the boy's spend part of their time learning the code so you can fix all this junk. That leaves us women trying to figure out what a barb on a fogger does and where it's located in the store."

"Shh. Not so loud. We can't let everyone in on the secret." Jeff hadn't felt the desire to laugh in—in—could it be eighteen years? He couldn't remember the last time he'd wanted to joke around.

She laughed. Beautiful, full, with the little snort at the end. "I knew it."

"Well, I would be honored, as a holder of the secrets, to assist you, my lady." He bowed at the waist.

Her head tipped, making more light sparkle in her hair. "You don't have to get your load to a job sight?"

"Just rebuilding a shed the last storm took down."

"I remember that storm. It was crazy." She turned and started walking, and he fell into step beside her as though they did this every day. "My neighbor had a thirty-foot pine nearly cleaved their house in two. No one got hurt, thank goodness, but our power was out for days."

"Wow. I thought I had it rough. I only lost the shed. Saved most of the tools inside."

"I had to throw out hamburger, cheese, and milk. I almost lost three cartons of ice cream." She rubbed her stomach and licked her lips.

"At least it wasn't a total loss." He chuckled both at her story and the fact she'd turned the wrong direction at the main aisle. "Plumbing's this way."

She glanced up at the department signs suspended from the ceiling. "Plumbing, right?"

"The floating arm?" She blinked. Her blue eyes reminded him of the sky at sunset. "The bar thingy attached to the floating thing in the toilet."

"Ah!"

Later as she made her purchases, and they headed out the door toward the cars, he stopped, pulling her up short. He extended his hand again. "Jeff, Jeff Tate."

She took it without reservation. "Jessica Easton."

"Thanks for taking the time to help and let me help you." He drew in a deep breath, and it eased out with a sigh. The next words came in little more than a whisper. "I really don't want it to end."

Jeff glanced at her from under his hood. His heart struggled to beat around the foreign emotions growing there. "Is there any way I could convince you to grab a smoothie with me?" He pointed to the shop at the far end of the parking lot and held his breath. This was insane. It couldn't go anywhere. But maybe, just maybe, she'd say yes. It would give him one happy memory, out of the last two decades of misery, to hang on to in the long lonely days ahead.

Chapter 2

His loneliness and self-imposed isolation had finally driven Jeff mad. Utterly off his rocker. He couldn't find another way to explain his need to spend time with Jessica. He'd just met this woman no more than thirty minutes ago, and he'd asked her out. Well, not on a date—but she might consider it a date. He hadn't been on one since before he married almost thirty years ago.

Jessica continued to smile as they strolled toward the smoothie shop. "You've purchased a lot of plywood. Your shed must be good-sized."

"It held all my tack and equipment. Would have stood longer if the termites and storm hadn't conspired together."

"Tack? Like in saddles?"

Jeff marveled at the fact she knew the term tack, but not float arm or emitter. "Yeah." They entered the smoothie shop and placed their orders. He paid.

"You don't have to pay, you know?"

"It's the least I can do for making you work so hard."

"You didn't make me do anything, and I enjoyed being useful." With their vivid colored drinks, they turned to the seating available. "It's too noisy in here." Jessica used her raised cup of deep red ice to point to a table outside. "You mind sitting out there?"

Mind? For whatever incomprehensible reason, Jeff would agree to sit on the moon to be with her for a few more moments. He should think about calling a psychologist. He didn't behave this way—not in the last eighteen years. He shook his head and held the door open for her.

She paused for a moment before she preceded him and moved to the table. She took the sunny side and left the chair under the full shade of the umbrella for him. The tiny cut-out metal table rocked as she set her drink down.

"Sure you don't want the shade?"

"Nah, the drink will make me cold." She lifted her cup in a toast and took a long draw on the straw. "Uh, cold freeze." She shuttered and sat it down again. Putting her foot up on one of the table's legs, she crossed her ankles, leaned back, and considered him with her warm grin. "Horses?"

Jeff settled onto the front of his heavy metal chair and rested his forearms on the table. "Yeah, I break difficult horses for others on a small ranch on the outskirts of Elk Grove. It's one of my jobs."

"One? How many do you have?"

"I work from home for a few different companies. Computer filing and management, billing, compiling analysis, and accounting. It allows me stay at home but pay the bills."

"I haven't ridden in years." She chuckled before she took another smaller drink. "I think the last time I rode a horse, my aunt and uncle were in town. My parents had taken us all to Lake Tahoe and we rented horses to ride near the shore. They were used to the trail and tourists, their heads hung as they plodded along—bored out of their minds. They barely swished their tails to keep the flies away. I think they called my uncle's horse, Oink."

She hadn't commented on him working at home. She offered no judgment, only the most comfortable conversation he'd ever had. "Those who come through my place are a little more spirited."

"How do you break them?"

"Slowly. With the damaged ones, trust doesn't come easy. Bad owners have screamed at, beaten, and whipped them. I'm sometimes the last stop before a gruesome end. Most of the original owners have turned them over to a place where they can serve as therapy animals. If I can't tame them to work well with people already suffering, they don't have any place to go but the glue factory."

"Do they still use horses for glue?"

Jeff chuckled. He'd said it often enough it sounded normal, but he could be repeating an old wives' tale. "You know, I have no idea."

"So, you're a horse whisperer?"

"I've been called that." Jeff raised his cup with a nod.

"Well, it's important work. The horses need someone to work them over their fears so they can help others with theirs."

"I never thought of it like that. The work is enjoyable and it pays the bills." He considered her again. Up to this point, they'd only talked about him. "And you? What do you do?"

She shrugged and took a long, slow drink. "Nothing as important or interesting as you. I work in a cube farm—an office full of cubicles, managing a group of *workers*—though I use the term loosely. We collect documents for review to distribute grant moneys allotted by the state."

"Some of those grants can be pretty important."

"But everyone wants money and there is little to show for it when it's all said and done. Nothing really changes."

"And your co-workers?"

"Oh, don't get me started. I'm going to church tomorrow and don't need to seek forgiveness yet again." Her words were full of mirth and mischief.

"I haven't been to church in years, I imagine, for as long as it's been since you've ridden."

"You should come. We're small but faithful, and we meet in Elk Grove." She pulled a pen from a pocket of her purse as it dangled from a decorative hook on the edge of the table, wrote the time and the address on her napkin, and handed it to him. "You're always welcome."

"Thanks." Jeff tucked it in his hoodie pocket. He had no intention of going. To come here, sit and drink smoothies with a woman, had already pulled him far outside his comfort-zone. He couldn't gather with a large group of people, and he was sure hoodies weren't allowed. Besides, God would never want him inside His house again.

They talked for a little while longer and sipped their drinks. When she slurped hers dry, her lips curved in disappointment. "Guess we have to return to our prospective homes and get to work on our projects."

"I suppose so." It helped to know she didn't seem to want to leave either. He stood and pulled out her chair as she rose. Again, she paused, and she gave him an odd look. He embodied his idea of a southern gentleman. This is what every man should do for a woman, but his action caused her to pause.

They trekked to their vehicles. "Thanks again for the assist," Jeff reached for her hand and inclined his head.

"It was my pleasure. Thanks for your help, too—and the smoothie. What a refreshing treat on such a hot day."

Jeff relinquished her hand and moved to his truck.

"Hope I'll see you tomorrow."

He shrugged. "Maybe."

Chapter 3

Jessica shook her head as she pulled out of the parking lot. "You have a confounding sense of humor, God. At the moment, I can't say I'm amused."

She turned down the praise music as she pulled onto the freeway. "I have prayed, begged, cried, screamed, and ranted—for years, about You bringing someone into my life. First a boyfriend, then a husband, then a friend, heck, any warm body to call when life and perspective turned bleakest, even someone for me to help to make me feel like my life matters. You have, nevertheless, remained silent on the matter of my companionship and need for connection with *some*body. This morning I gave up. Surrendered to it being You and me and then You go and do this? What are You up to? And do I even want to know?"

Jessica had put off the trip to the home improvement store for over a week. As the lawn turned browner by the day, she decided she'd lose it for good if she didn't get the sprinklers fixed. With a sigh, she'd risen from her defeated prayer on her knees—something she never did—and headed out the door. A huge flatbed had blocked her normal entrance into the parking lot. She had to go to the far end closest to the garden department. The lot sat almost full except for a couple of spots at the end of one row next to a man struggling by himself to load an entire cart of plywood.

Jessica remained in her car and watched him battle with a single large sheet before she'd looked up with her finger pointed at heaven. "Now! Seriously? It's like a thousand degrees outside today, and You want me to help him load wood? Oh, Your timing stinks."

She shook her head again, this time at herself. She knew good and well the name of a float arm and where to locate the sprinkler parts. Okay, she didn't know it was called a bobbing fogger, but she knew what they looked like and where to find them. She'd played dumb because she wanted him to rescue her, which made absolutely no sense. Jessica had been doing repairs around her place by herself for decades. She knew every aisle of the home improvement store but let him play the hero. Jessica had no idea why.

She pulled into her garage and sat in her car as the door lowered behind her. In the dim light, the image of his terrified gaze captured her again. Jeff had looked as though he feared for his life when his hood blew off. Sure, he had a scar, probably from a burn, but it wasn't bad. Smooth, light skin stretched over a little of his neck and kissed his jaw. He hadn't been grossly disfigured, but Jeff acted ashamed of his wounds —or at least what had caused them. His reaction to being uncovered made it clear.

Jessica hadn't been able to determine his eye color as his pupils had engulfed the irises. He wore his hair cut neat and not too long or super short. The black locks had been straight and ruffled by his hood. His oval face had high cheekbones. Though he'd hidden in his hoodie today, his skin had a deep sun-kissed tone.

Still, from the jerk and release of her hand, to the tremor that had run through him, the man leaked fear like a broken radiator spewed precious coolant.

Jessica stepped from her car at last. The girls were clamoring at the door for her to come in the house. Their nails were sure to remove all the paint if she didn't open the barrier to the kitchen soon. Her two chihuahua mixes were the only thing that kept her sane most days.

She thought about Jeff and his small scar again. Scars were a part of this life, it seemed. Some came by them in accidents, others by more shameful means. She rubbed her leg.

Chapter 4

Heat licked at exposed flesh. Pain tore up my arm. The stench of burned skin seared my nose. A child wailed.

Jeff jerked upright, freeing himself of another flashback. He sat on the side of his bed and reached for the bucket he always kept nearby. It had been bad this time. The charred smell hadn't evaporated with the nightmare, and he vomited.

How much longer can I endure this hell?

Tonight's violent retching continued unabated. It hadn't been this bad in a couple of years—other than on the anniversary of that terrible night. Jessica's smiling face flashed in his mind. His stomach heaved long after it was empty and the effort fruitless.

He'd thought about her all afternoon as he unloaded the wood on a wheeled cart and started cutting it to fit the waiting frame of two-by-fours. But remembering her now made him queasy.

He tried to picture her scowling face as it filled with disgust when she learned what he'd done, but her image continued to smile at him. Jeff imagined the impossible. She'd hate him if she ever learned of his past.

But it didn't matter. He'd never see her again. It was better this way. A happy memory unmarred by his horrible actions. At last the exhausting dry heaves abated, and he rested on the edge of his bed. The smell in his room and the lingering taste in his mouth drove him to the bathroom.

After emptying and cleaning the bucket, he brushed his teeth. Now wide-awake and unwilling for an encore of his nightmare, he moved to the living room. A chill slithered over his bare arms and chest though the heat from the day still warmed the house. He snatched up his hoodie and moved toward the couch.

His fingers played with the rough texture of a flimsy scrap in his pocket. He drew out the buff-colored napkin. He unfolded it to revealed neat bubbly writing that mirrored her personality, open and pretty:

Rivers of Grace, 9:30, 1525 Wellington Lane.

Reaching for the remote, he tried to ignore the summons. He wouldn't find much on at two a.m. He could stream an old series or a favorite movie—anything to get his mind off the distant past and his encounter today. He wanted to crush the napkin in his fist. They would never accept him there. How could they welcome a man like him?

"The Lord is calling you!"

Jeff startled as his TV came to life. A preacher stood behind a carved wooden pulpit; his Bible held high in the air. "The Lord wants you—" he hit the remote. An info-mercial about a newfangled car cleaner filled the screen. He closed his eyes and tried to catch his breath. His empty hand made his eyes pop open again. The napkin had fallen to the floor.

The pretty handwriting staring back at him came with her voice, 'You should come.' Her gentle beckon added to the preacher's shout of the Lord calling him until it clamored in his weary brain in a ruckus cacophony. He leaned back, rested his head on the couch, and stared at the ceiling sure he would vomit again.

Jeff sat in his pickup, as his hands gripped the steering wheel in a strangle hold. He'd never gone back to bed, because he didn't want a revisit of the old memory. Still, the notion of attending Jessica's church wouldn't let him be either. He couldn't remember a time he suffered such badgering.

"I don't want to be here," he said again as he stared at the cross over the entrance, but he didn't feel free to return home. He glanced down at the only pair of khaki's he owned. They were a little tight, but the rest of his wardrobe consisted of jeans. He didn't own a suit or a dress jacket. Jeff stared in the rearview mirror at his one non-plaid shirt. The off blue color clashed with his lone green tie. He propped the collar up in an eighties preppy style. He didn't know of any other way to cover his scars, and the collar didn't do the job well.

Without releasing his death grip on the steering wheel, Jeff glanced at his watch—9:20. He scanned the parking lot again. He didn't see Jessica's SUV. Could she have another car? Maybe she wouldn't attend today. But it he couldn't miss her. The long narrow lot consisted of four rows. He'd backed into a spot in the row nearest the street, a fair distance from the church entrance to watch for Jessica.

The building looked to be an old strip mall. It might have held a half dozen or more little shops at one time. Now the church occupied one end with a couple of medical offices in the rest.

"I don't want to be here."

He tried to roll his tight shoulders.

9:24.

An SUV pulled in the middle row and parked facing the church also, about a dozen cars to his right.

A familiar woman with gold streaks rippling through her hair stepped out. She'd pulled it back near her temples in a clip. Her brilliant white blouse fluttered as she pushed the car door closed, but she didn't move. Her head and her shoulders drooped. After a moment, she glanced up at the gleaming cross and took a few slow steps. Nothing of the life and spark remained from yesterday.

What could be bothering her?

A woman sped up the sidewalk in front of Jessica. The gal said something, Jessica's head turned his way as she looked up and offered a weak smile and wave to the passing woman. But her slow, labored steps persisted as the other lady continued past her and Jessica stared at the ground again. She paused at the door, hand on the bar, a deep rise and fall of her shoulders before she pulled it open.

Jeff slid out of the truck, crossed the lot, and stepped onto the sidewalk before he comprehended any action. Inside the cool building, a large open space greeted him with a smattering of potted plants and a few small seating areas. A little coffee bar sat tucked in the corner. Someone sat behind the counter on the opposite wall. To the left, a couple stood passing out papers and greeting people in front of propped open double doors that led into the sanctuary beyond.

People milled about and engaged in lively discussion. Jessica stood alone near the back. She watched the shrinking crowd as they filed through the double doors, and Jeff kept his eyes on her. His heart thudded. He stood inside a church—somewhere he swore he'd never go again. The building hadn't collapsed on his head yet—a surprising revelation. Still, he'd come for one reason. Jessica drew him like iron to a magnet. He wiped his sweaty palms on his thighs and fought for a deep breath.

He approached her and cleared his throat.

"Oh, sorry." She stepped back out of the way to let him pass between her and a chair before she looked his direction. Their eyes met. But she gave no reaction. *What am I doing here?*

Chapter 5

Jessica's eyes widened, and her mouth opened. In one sudden movement, she threw her arms around Jeff's neck. "Oh my gosh. You came." She released him with a quick jerk and her cheeks flared bright with color. "I'm glad you're here." Her smile grew full and genuine.

"Yeah." Her exuberant embrace left him reeling, and his mouth failed to work or his brain to form thought.

"Oh, I'm sorry." She reached for his tie, worked the knot loose, and removed it. "I should have said we're pretty casual here." Jessica undid the top two buttons of his shirt and laid down the collar. Her hand brushed his scar. Everything in his experience told Jeff to run, yet every muscle in his body refused to twitch. Not only had she glimpsed his hideous disfigurement, now she exposed him to the scorn of the world. If he could just move, he'd escape. What was wrong with him?

In truth, the pressure against the unfeeling surface was the first time anyone had touched him since he'd left the infirmary. Could it be some deep need for human contact that caused his immobility?

Jessica didn't flinch or cringe. She brushed down his shoulders and arms before stepping back to appraise him. "Perfect." Her eyes sparkled with merriment.

How could she call his marred flesh, faultless?

She slipped to his side as she rolled his tie into a nice bundle and dropped it in a pocket in her purse. He followed her light and bouncing steps. She took an offered pamphlet from the woman at the door as a voice spoke over the microphone inside.

"Good morning, Jess." The woman greeted her. About thirty with brown hair, she wore a calf-length skirt and form-fitting blouse. She hugged Jessica.

After the embrace, Jessica turned and motioned toward him. "This is my friend, Jeff."

Jeff startled at her referring to him as more than an acquaintance.

The man at the other door shook Jeff's gloved hand and offered him a brochure. He wore khakis too, and a Hawaiian print shirt. "Welcome."

"Thank you." This man didn't stare at his scars either. He offered a warm and inviting smile. Jeff relaxed by another degree. Maybe coming wouldn't turn out as bad as he feared.

The woman passing out papers hugged Jeff too, before he followed Jessica through the doors. Two embraces in the last eighteen years, and they'd both happened in the previous two minutes. His head whirled.

Jessica directed him past an older couple and took the seat between him and the elderly lady in polyester slacks and a heavy sweater. Jessica's elbow pressed lightly against his right arm, but she didn't shy away from him.

Jeff looked around as someone read the announcements. The room formed a square with the stage in one corner opposite the inner doors they'd come through. Padded chairs of deep red filled the space in neat rows. A large main aisle went down the center with two smaller ones on either side. Where were the pews? An accordion curtain sat cracked open beside them. It revealed more chairs inside. By Jeff's quick count, about a hundred were present this morning. But only one held his attention.

Jessica bowed her head. When it came up again, tears glistened and teetered on her lids. "Thank you for coming." He almost missed her quiet whisper.

The performers on stage play the first notes, drawing his attention. A bass, electric, and acoustic guitars, a couple keyboards and drums backed up the three singers. No organ. Church had changed a lot.

They rose as words shone on screens on the wall on either side of the stage. They sang of God's goodness, His forgiveness, and the healing found in His scars. Jeff tried to concentrate, but again Jessica dominated his attention.

Her eyes closed, and she sang out with bold confidence. At times, her right hand rose toward the ceiling.

After the first song, the congregation stopped to greet one another. He received a few more hugs, and shook many hands. They all said they were glad he'd come when Jessica introduced him. She beamed, and he couldn't imagine her smile could be any larger.

Jeff lost track of how many songs they sang before they sat, and the pastor began to preach. He didn't speak from the stage behind a pulpit but on the floor. He wandered a few steps to either side of the main aisle and back. A well-loved Bible lay open in his hand. He also wore khakis and a Hawaiian print shirt. His gray hair hung in short waves. Jeff found his rich voice both commanding and filled with kindness.

The preacher spoke on God's love for all people. Jessica diligently took notes from the overhead screens, while her phone, with a Bible app open to their passage, balanced on her knee.

The words *all* and *everyone* were emphasized several times. The pastor focused his comments in Jeff's direction more than once. The service ended with another song, as the offering basket passed along the rows. Jessica snatched it before he could get anything out of his pocket. She smiled at him as the song concluded.

Jessica made sure to introduce him to anyone they passed as they moved toward the doors and out into the foyer. Jessica and the pastor exchanged a side hug. "Pastor Matt, this is Jeff. Jeff, this is our pastor, Matthew Moss."

The preacher shook his hand and gave him a quick hug. "Welcome. We're glad you came."

"Thank you."

Jeff and Jessica moved closer to the doors leading outside, but the waves of heat wafting off the blacktop kept them inside. Or maybe something else prevented them from parting.

"I don't think I have ever been hugged this much in my entire life." Jeff stared at the shimmering waves of heat rippling outside. No one had recoiled from him or seemed to take notice of his scars.

"We're a huggy bunch."

Jeff looked at her.

A little of her smile had faded. "Thank you again for coming."

"I enjoyed it. It's not anything like I remember church being. It's more …"

"Relaxed?"

"Yeah, maybe a little. But there was something else. Can't quite describe it."

"Well, I hope you'll come again." She bit a corner of her lower lip.

Jeff nodded, but clamped his mouth closed. They hadn't thrown him out, but he still didn't belong here. In fact, he'd fought all morning not to attend. Jeff couldn't imagine returning, but then who knew what would happen if the holy harassment continued.

The crowd thinned and Jessica's smile dimmed a little more.

"You want to grab some lunch?" The words were out of his mouth before he knew he intended to say them. Jeff felt like he had lost control of his own body. He avoided people, yet here he stood in church, with a woman he knew he could never have a relationship with, fighting to spend more time with her. If he prolonged his connection to her, it would inevitably set him up for misery in the near future. But he couldn't seem to put the brakes on the situation.

Her smile brightened. "There are a few places the next block down." She named them, and they agreed on an all-American diner. "You can follow me." Her steps had a bounce as she moved to the door. Jeff pushed it open as she reached for it and again it gave her pause. He followed her to her car and opened her door when she pressed the button to unlock it. She stopped and stared at him. Jessica acted like no one had ever done that before.

"My truck is at the end."

"Perfect. It's easier to get out there anyway."

She stepped in and he closed the door behind her. She offered him a lopsided smile.

Jeff ambled to his car. He liked Jessica and regretted knowing it would never work out for them to be together more than this one day.

Chapter 6

"What? Am I still sixteen again?" Jessica berated herself as her vehicle idled in front of Jeff's truck and waited for him to pull out to follow. "I'm nearing fifty, not a swooning teenager. But I'm a complete mess. One glimpse of him and I turn into a babbling idiot. The mere sight of a man I'd met once less than twenty-four hours ago, and I threw myself at him. Then, in the church foyer, I undressed him, removed his tie and undid two shirt buttons. I'm not sure if I was more surprised he'd allowed me to do it, or at the horror in his eyes."

Jeff pulled out behind her. "Lord, what is happening to me? And *what* are You doing?"

She waited until the traffic cleared enough for the both of them to enter the street.

He'd come because she'd asked. Her mind kept repeating the thought. No one had ever attended church with her, though she'd invited many. But Jeff had come. All dressed in a pressed shirt and a tie. Sure, they didn't match and the tie's style was out of date. But he'd made a major effort. She glanced at her purse in the passenger's seat. She still had his tie.

They parked at the restaurant and somehow Jeff exited his truck and had her door open before she could collect herself. More proof of what a hot mess she was at the moment. No one ever opened doors for her. What a gentleman. Old school. Thoughtful.

He inclined his head as she returned his tie and slid out. "Thanks. Forgot all about it."

Wish I could forget it. I'll be reliving the embarrassingly awkward moment for weeks.

He tossed it in his truck as they passed and entered the restaurant.

Sunday after church, the eatery looked pretty full. Jessica didn't eat out unless she got it to go. It made her more miserable to sit alone in public.

"We have a few spots at the bar if you don't want to wait," the hostess said.

The vein in Jeff's neck reminded her of one on the Hulk. His eyes were wide.

"How long until we can be seated?" Jessica said.

After a quick scan of the list of names, the host looked back at them. "About twenty to twenty-five minutes."

"We can wait," Jessica said.

Jeff's shoulders relaxed by a couple of inches as they moved to the waiting area and found a spot to stand out of the way. "Thank you."

"The bar's not very comfortable, and it's hard to hear," Jessica said with a shrug.

"You eat at the bar often?" An odd edge tainted his words.

"No, it's where you wait to pick up to-go orders. I don't eat out much."

"Maybe we need to change that."

Jessica turned and stared at him. *Did mischief flicker in his milk chocolate eyes? Impossible. I have no experience with men. He can't be into me. No one ever is. But he came here with me, even after I decimated all social boundaries this morning.*

His smile curved into a smirk. "Is it such a bad idea?"

"A foreign one, but not bad."

They moved several times as others were called and new people joined them to wait.

Jessica fought for something—anything to say. "Thanks again for coming today. I hope you enjoyed it."

"I like your singing."

Oh, stink! Seriously? Heat seared her entire body. "Sorry about the racket." Her hands clamped together, head down. "Bible says we can make a joyful noise. It's the best I can do."

"But I liked it."

"You are a very nice man."

"Jessica?" They turned and followed a hostess to a table.

She scanned the menu, hiding behind it to get a grip on her crazed thoughts and rampaging emotions.

"Can I get some drinks started?"

Jessica jumped at the intrusion. She'd thought the woman had left. "Lemonade?"

"Coke," Jeff said, though his gaze remained fixed on Jessica. "Anything particularly good here?" he asked when the hostess had left.

His frequent glances were distracting. *What's he see in me? Why does he keep staring?* He'd watched her in church, too.

"You all right?"

"Yeah," she glanced at the menu and listed some of her favorites. "I'm going to have the stir-fry today."

A young waiter came to take their order.

"May we have separate checks?"

"There's no need," Jeff corrected her.

"You don't have to—" They discussed who'd pay as the waiter shifted his weight between his feet. When was the last time anyone had bought her—anything? Her parents on her birthday?

"Give me the bill. I'll have the rib-eye." Jeff listed his desired sides and the finish of his meat while Jessica floated on a wave of disbelief. She expected to wake at any moment and have to go to church alone— or worse, work.

Jessica failed to place her order, as she waited to wake up.

"Didn't you say you wanted the stir-fry?" Jeff tipped his head, and he considered her with a long stare.

"Yeah," she nodded and answered the waiter's questions on specifics, but Jeff continued to watch her.

"You know you act like you've never been out with anyone before."

He hadn't said date, thankfully, but heat flooded her cheeks nonetheless. *Think woman! Turn the questions back to him.* She took a quick sip of her drink. "Did you get all your plywood unloaded?"

"I have a tall cart with wheels. Slid the sheets out onto it and pushed it beside the shed. I almost have one wall completed."

"Wow, you're fast. Shouldn't take you anytime to finish."

"I'll work some more this afternoon if it doesn't get unbearably hot."

Their conversation lagged. She sucked at keeping small talk going. Thankfully, the food arrived.

Elbows off the table.

Small dainty bites.

Don't rush.

Oh, who are you kidding? Just take most of it home and don't make any more of a fool of yourself than you have already. You are such a loser.

Chapter 7

Jeff again sat in Rivers of Grace's parking lot and looked for Jessica's car. It'd been three weeks since he'd made his one visit. He glanced at the cross after a third check of the time. 9:29. "I still say I don't belong here." At least if he went home, he was in his jeans and could go right to work. Today he wore a western shirt and left the top couple of buttons open and the collar down.

Shame he'd never been bold enough to get her number. He reached to turn the key when she drove in. She didn't hurry though the service had started. He came alongside her as they stepped into the foyer and bumped shoulders with her. "Hey."

She didn't look up. "You came back?" No hug today.

"Yeah."

She stopped before they made it to the sanctuary doors and the waiting brochures. "Whatever I did, I'm sorry."

"You didn't do a thing."

"Then I'm sorry I didn't do *something*," she muttered.

"Jessica?" The music began, and she moved before he could get any answers.

She glanced his way. "Are you limping?"

"Yeah, maybe I'll tell you about it at lunch?" Now she looked at him. Wide eyes, brimming with tears met his gaze. "Come on, I'm missing your singing," Jeff said.

They slipped in next to the elderly couple again. After the first song, the congregation greeted one another. He finally got a timid hug from her. As the second number began, Jeff leaned into her. "I really do enjoy your singing, and I can't hear you." Jessica didn't get much louder, and she never raised her hand.

Once they sat, Jeff noted she circled something in a flyer from her bulletin and then added it to her phone. He glanced at his insert when her attention turned to the preacher. A notice invited the congregation to join a work day next Saturday. They wanted to help rebuild a fellow member's house after a fire damaged the garage and a couple of rooms.

Jeff marked it and then struggled to concentrate on Pastor Matt. Jessica had helped him with a huge load of lumber and had bubbled over with friendliness. He'd twice sat and talked with her, and it was the most comfortable and natural thing he could ever remember doing. She'd been glad to see him the first Sunday. Now she seemed—frightened? Self-conscious? Maybe she had no feeling for him and regretted seeing him again. He had only met her twice before, but he knew something seemed off.

The last song ended and Jeff eased up on his sore leg. "Same place? Or should we try something new?"

"You were serious about lunch?"

"Of course? Jessica, are you all right?"

"I didn't think you'd ever come again."

"How else could I tell you about the insane couple of weeks I've had?" He followed her through the foyer, and they greeted Pastor Matt.

"Jeff, glad to see you."

The pastor had remembered his name—impressive. "Thanks."

"Have a great week and I look forward to seeing you next Sunday."

Jeff nodded. He'd like to say he wouldn't be back, but his wishes weren't going as he planned recently.

They went to a Chinese place Jessica favored this time and ordered family style. "Tell me what happened."

Jeff ran his fingers through his hair. "The first Sunday, a couple weeks ago, I had no intention of ever stepping in a church again. I don't belong. But I wanted to see you and couldn't get the notion of church off my mind and after waking up at two a.m. it continued to nag me. I knew it had been the right decision when I saw you again. You made my week—heck, my entire decade."

"I'm nothing special."

"You sell yourself short." He considered her for a long moment. She studied her clasped hands and didn't look at him. "I couldn't believe the events of that first week after meeting you. New clients for the online business, a new horse who has been a dream to train. Nothing went wrong. But I couldn't bring myself to step inside a church again."

"Why not?"

"You don't know anything about me, Jessica."

"A hospital isn't for healthy people, and a church is the same. We don't go because we're worthy. We go because we're lost, broken, fallen, and need a loving Savior."

Jeff had never considered it like that. He nodded. "Though I couldn't get you out of my head, I chose not to go. Then the next week when I didn't come, my computer got the mother of all viruses. Lost a week getting it disinfected. Got another horse who still won't come near me. Lost one client and had another one give me a crazy load with an unreasonable deadline. Last Sunday, when I should have been in church with you, the mean-spirited demon horse kicked me."

Jessica gasped.

"I'm lucky she didn't make a direct hit. But instead of enjoying another lunch with you, I spent the entire day in the ER getting a dozen stitches. The rest of the week hasn't gone much better. Now, I'm testing a theory. If this week goes well, I'll know God has been behind all this."

"He wants us to know Him. Even when we don't feel like we belong."

"Well, there is definitely an upside." He looked at Jessica with a smirk.

"I'm sure there are many."

He tipped his head and winked at her. "Only one matters."

"God."

Jeff sighed. "You."

Her eyes widened and her cheeks pinked. She looked away again. "God should be more important."

Possibly, yet an all-consuming force drew him to Jessica. Everything would change though, when she learned the truth. She'd understand then why God wouldn't welcome him inside His house. The thought caught. He'd been in church twice and nothing had happened to him. Lightening hadn't flashed from heaven to strike him down. If he proved his theory this next week, what would that mean about how God felt of him?

He shook off his musings as the food came and their conversation turned to other interests—his. She didn't talk about herself much.

Chapter 8

Jessica growled. *When am I going to develop the emotional maturity of someone over the age of fifteen? Seriously, is it any wonder no one's into me?*

She'd been stunned when Jeff had joined her at church the first week, and heartbroken when he didn't return. Now he was back, and she'd almost skipped attending herself today. He'd come, but not because of her. He came to make deals with God. 'I'll go to church and God, You provide me a good week.' God didn't bargain. *At least He doesn't with me.*

The girls, her two were jumping against her legs as she tried to enter the house. She put the left overs in the fridge. Jeff had paid again. *For someone not into me, he's doing everything to prove otherwise.* She considered the idea for a while.

Sitting on the couch the girls leapt in her lap and tried to lick her face. "All right you two, get it out of your system. I have chores to do." They wouldn't leave until she pushed them off, and she didn't. When she finished her Sunday tasks, it meant she'd head for bed and have to get up and go work in the morning. *How many times have I told you, God, the depth of loathing I have for my job?*

"Jess, I need you," Kevin, her supervisor, said as her soles hit the carpet of the office workspace.

Yolanda poked her flaming-red head out of her cubicle. Her eyes were caked in layers of make-up "Jessica? This file won't open."

Jessica marveled at the woman's ability to get logged on each day. Between her lack of skill and outrageously long nails, Jessica wondered how she had managed to get hired anywhere.

"Jessica, have you seen the grant request from Richland Christian?" Bert, a short man with thinning hair, proved to be their most competent employee, which didn't say much. Her dogs could get about the same done in a day as this bunch.

"People!" Jessica barked. "Can I get to my desk and put my purse away before you assault me, please?"

"You are harassing me." Ian stood next to Yolanda's cubicle and had been talking to her. The super-slender man with rarely-washed, stringy hair was on the spectrum of something. Jessica grew to expect the unexpected from him on any given day.

"I'm not harassing you. Everyone is harassing *me.*"

Ian's voice rose and his arms flailed over his head. "You accused me of assault. I have not touched you. I've never attacked anyone. You can look in my permanent record. I am not violent and you cannot accuse me of hurting you. You are filing a false report. It is against the law to file a false report."

Jessica hung her head and lumbered to her cubicle in the center of the room. She'd triggered the man, and this Monday morning hadn't really started. Oh, the week ahead looked to be a bear.

"Jess?"

"I'm coming," she dropped her purse in her file draw and locked it.

She passed Ian still consumed in his tirade. He backed away from her, waved his hands like he warded off an attack. It'd be an hour at least before he could settle and get to work—if he didn't register a formal complaint with HR or call the police. He had done either, and both.

"The file?" Yolanda asked.

Jessica veered from her destination and double-clicked on the attachment and then hit download.

"Jessica, the Richland file?" Bert said.

She stopped there too and opened her email in Bert's inbox and clicked on the desired communication.

"Oh, sorry. Don't know how I missed it."

She finally neared Kevin's office. The glass front walls revealed he sat behind his desk waiting for her. The remainder of his space was painted with the only color in the entire building other than pallor gray—though beige wasn't much of a step up on the color spectrum. His office also had a window and nice lights, not the hideous flickering iridescent ones causing her eye strain.

Ravi almost collided with her at the door. "I see Mr. Perry. Most important." The man always skipped her in the chain of command and went straight to Kevin. Between her gender and her religion, Ravi had no use for her.

"You know you can't see him until you have spoken to me first."

His lip curled in a snarl. "I speak to Mr. Perry. I don't need you, Jess."

"Well, he has asked to see me; you will have to wait."

"This is most important." He shouldered her aside to enter.

She followed him into Kevin's office.

"What do you need, Ravi?"

He looked at Jessica. "Mr. Perry is busy. Ravi will come back later." He pushed into her on his way out too.

Jessica dropped into the chair in front of the desk. "You know he skipped me again."

"I'll deal with him later. I need the quarterly reports for our meeting this afternoon."

"They are your responsibility."

"I delegated them to you."

"It's not in my job description, as well you know. We've had this discussion many times, the last time in Vicki's office." Their manager had defined the tasks each of them would be responsible for, and all but one report was assigned to him.

"But I don't know how to do them."

"I have shown you each time they've come around for the last eighteen months. You have to step it up and do these jobs for yourself. I won't always be here." She was at least twenty years older than him. His obvious inability or refusal to complete his own responsibilities added yet another example to her growing list of reasons why she couldn't wait to quit this nightmare of a job. She'd trained him, but he continued to rely on her to do much of his job.

"You keep threatening you'll quit. I don't believe you. Now, I need you to do the report this quarter and I'll do it next time. The meeting is in three hours. I won't have time."

"Neither will I."

"If we look bad at the meeting, they'll know whose fault it is." Kevin leaned back in his chair and entwined his fingers over his muffin-top belly. He gave her a quick nod and the short light brown stubble stood on end as his jaw set.

"Yes, yours, as you are the office manager."

"Heads will roll, Jessica." Kevin only called her by her full name when she'd irritated him.

"I can only pray it will be mine." She stood and leaned over his desk. "I'll get you started, but I'm not doing it."

"Jess, have a heart." Now he tried to sweet talk her.

"I can't do your job and mine too. Not with the slackers we have around here." This really was going to be a sucky week.

Chapter 9

Jessica logged out of the time clock app and turned off her screen. 4:55 p.m. She was overdone. As she'd predicted it'd been a week from the pit. Ian had called the cops and claimed his coworkers had implanted surveillance devices to his teeth. Yolanda crashed her workstation once and later in the week the entire network for an hour. In the end, Jessica had been forced to write the quarterly report and then reprimanded for not completing her own assignments.

She moved to the break room to collect her assortment of containers from the week. Five more minutes, and she could escape for a couple of days. *What would happen if I didn't come back on Monday? Is there anything important in my cubicle I'd be leaving behind?* No, she didn't have pictures of anyone, no plants. As a flora serial killer, she had the blackest thumbs on record.

"Jess?" Kevin called from his office, and she moved out of sight of the doorway.

Not now. I have three minutes left until freedom.

"Yolanda, have you seen Jess?"

"No, sir. Maybe she left early. Her computer's off."

Jessica held her breath as Kevin asked the others. Two minutes. *Please, I want to go home.*

Kevin poked his head a little way into the break room but not far enough to see her.

One more minute.

"She couldn't have left without me seeing her. Jess?" His call echoed through the section.

Thirty seconds. One of her protein shake containers teetered in her grasp, caught on her elbow, tipped back on the pile in her arms, and somersaulted over her other arm. Next it hit the counter, ricocheted into her stack, and knocked three more cups loose. They all hit a chair, spun across the tabletop, slammed into the saltshaker, and jettisoned it against the door until finally, the salt, drink containers, and almost everything left in her hands landed on the floor with a clatter.

"Mr. Kevin, Jessica is throwing dishes around the break room," Ian said.

"Jess, there you are. Didn't you hear me call you?"

"I had my head in the fridge." She lied—and she didn't care.

"Well, there is something you need to do before you leave."

"Kevin, the week is over. It will have to wait until Monday."

"The supervisor needs the cost analysis of the Foundation Grant payout first thing Monday."

"Cost analyses are your job." She started to gather up her scattered containers and throw them in a bag.

"I didn't have time."

"Well, neither do I. It's after five."

Kevin turned and waved the others a good evening. "I'll expect the report on my desk on Monday."

"No!" She wanted to reach in her bag and throw each container at his head. "I have plans for this weekend and I will not work overtime on a report assigned to you."

"Jessica, you know how the supervisors reacts when we aren't prepared."

She drew in a deep breath.

"Good. I'll see you Monday."

She followed him out. "Kevin, you can fire me, but I am not staying alone to do your job." She headed for the door.

"Now, wait a minute. You can't leave me hanging like this."

"I'm not doing anything to you. I've done my job. Time for you to do your own."

"Fine, do whatever it is you have planned for the weekend. You can come in early Monday and do it then."

"Good night, Kevin." Jessica's heart hammered as she fled down the stairs and into the dark parking garage. After watching hours of crime dramas, this place unnerved her. She made it a habit to leave with everyone else. But Kevin had delayed her, and now only the sound of her echoing footsteps accompanied her. If no one murdered or kidnapped her on the way to her car, she hoped she'd get fired on Monday and be free of this place. *But what else can I do? Who would hire me at my age?*

Chapter 10

Jessica pulled up to the Hansen's home on the other side of Elk Grove the next morning. She needed to do something to feel useful, valuable, important. In all honesty, she hoped she could smash some nails in the walls of this rebuild.

A dispute over the cause of the electrical fire continued. It had gutted the kitchen and part of the living room and garage. The insurance company dragged out payment, and the Hansens didn't have anywhere to go.

"Good morning, Jessica." David greeted her with a wave. "The women are preparing food out back."

"I'd like to be of help inside."

David drew up short and looked at her with a high arched brow.

"Give me a chance. If you don't like my work, I'll totter off to the women's corner."

She picked up one end of the drywall, and they carried it inside.

"I didn't mean to disparage your abilities, Jessica," David said with a kind smile. "My wife and daughter often join me on a project. But I believe today is the first time I've ever heard you say a word. Well, other than, 'Hello.'" He shook his head. "No. You only wave."

Did I find my problem? I don't know anyone or have any friends, because I've never had the guts to be bold enough to open my mouth. David and she carried the drywall sheet into the kitchen and held it against the studs. He used the drill first and then handed it to her. As she pulled the trigger and drove in each screw, something clicked in her. Resolve set in. *Be bold!* She would make it her new motto. *Be bold, Jessica,* she admonished herself. *I've lived most of my life as a cowering wuss. No more. Today I will do what I have always wanted. Say what needs to be said.*

As they moved back to the driveway to collect the next sheet, Jessica looked at David. "I've decided it's time to be bold."

"Good for you."

After a couple more sheets, someone asked David to assist in another area of the house. "Dylan?" David called. "Dylan." He looked around inside a bit before he moved to the backyard. "Dylan!"

"Geez, what?" David's son, a sixteen-year-old with dyed black hair, long on top and short on the sides, walked in. He had an earbud in one ear and his gaze riveted to the phone screen in his hand.

David snatched the device and the earbuds as his son looked up. "Hey."

"Don't 'hey' me. If you want me to sign off on your community service hours to make up points for your Bible class, you won't have this for the rest of the day. You still intend to complete the class, right?" He waved the phone in the air and Dylan nodded. "Then you *will* help."

"Whatever."

"Go help Miss Jessica bring in more drywall." David turned to her. "You know the plan, right?"

"Got it." Jessica gave him a thumbs up and Dylan followed her out to the garage, dragging his steps.

They had just picked up the next piece when Dylan lost his grip and it started to fall. A man in a dark sweatshirt and one glove shoved the teenager out of the way and snatched it before the sheet broke.

She adjusted the weight and secured its hold in her hands before she looked up to see her hero.

Jeff smiled. "Hey."

"Hey." She swallowed and tried to wet her suddenly parched mouth as her stomach flipped. *Be bold.*

Chapter 11

Jeff pulled up to the address from the flyer in the bulletin. Jessica worked hard already. Her long denim shorts and yellow T-shirt were sprinkled with drywall dust. She'd arranged her hair in a small ponytail and clip to keep it off her neck and out of her eyes. The sight of her hit him with a jolt. Four times. He had seen her exactly four separate times in the last six weeks. But something drew him to her. He thought about her day and night, counted the minutes until he could spend time with her again. He'd come today to be with her—before Sunday service and lunch came around. Another opportunity to breathe the same air as Jessica Easton—being next to her would have to be enough. "But I want more," he whispered.

A stack of drywall sat in the garage and, like with his plywood, she worked to move it. Jessica picked up one end and a high school kid in sagging shorts struggled to lift the other side.

Jeff slipped out of his pickup and pushed up the left sleeve of his hoodie. The heat already weighed him down at this hour of the morning. If the weather had started out this hot in June, the rest of the summer could prove to be miserable.

The kid caught his toe on the remaining stack and stumbled as Jessica backed toward the house. Jeff snatched the sheet before the young man lost his grip and dropped it.

Jessica stared at him.

"Hey."

"Hey," she said, but still didn't move. Her brows pinched together. "What are you doing here?"

"I can read a bulletin too. I saw you circle this event and put it in your phone."

Her face scrunched up in even deeper confusion. "You knew I'd be here?"

"It's why I came."

"You … you came for me?"

He smiled and nodded as he swallowed his fear and forced himself to be forthright. "I'm enjoying our time together. Is that so strange?"

"Well … yes," she stammered. "I don't endear many people to stick around long."

"Until now."

She stared at him as if trying to determine an alternative motive or the joke he played on her.

"We going someplace with this?"

She glanced down, as if noticing the heavy sheet in their hands for the first time, nodded, and finally backed up.

Jeff marveled at her hidden strength. They tipped the large sheet on its side to go through the doorway. The back of the garage, kitchen, and family room took the worst of the damage. Jeff shot a quick, 'thank you' to the heavens because no sight or smell of the fire remained. He didn't want to trigger another flashback. Instead, he found fresh framing waiting for their drywall. They moved it into a spot under the ceiling sheets already in place. Three sheets were secured overhead of where they stood this one. Jessica picked up the drill. She fixed this latest panel to the studs closest to her and handed it to him to do his side.

"Okay, color me impressed."

"I'm not your average dumb blond."

Jeff wanted to come back with, 'So, you're an above average dumb blond?' but he doubted Jessica would ever be ready for his snarky tongue. "Never thought you were dumb," he said instead.

They stepped back and considered their next move. "David said to work with his son on the walls until he came back and we could finish the ceiling."

"Yeah, the ceiling is usually done first. But you're right, the kid would have struggled to lift these overhead if he couldn't even carry it in from the garage. Is David the homeowner?"

She grabbed the tape measure and calculated the remaining gap in the ceiling near the back wall. "No, he's the worship leader. He's also a general contractor who put this work crew together. It will take us a couple of weekends at least, and we don't even know if the insurance will come through to cover the cost. They say an overloaded outlet caused the fire. The Hansens say they never used the plug-in question and usually all the other outlets were free in the kitchen."

"We are forced to have insurance for when 'The Terrible' raises its ugly head, but the same company will fight like a badger protecting a burrow not to pay."

"True." She finished her measuring and stood with her fists on her hips. "Dang."

"What's wrong?"

"Looks like we have another full sheet. Then the next one is only three and a quarter foot near the wall and three and a half in the middle of the room."

"Old homes often have wonky walls. We'll have to cut the last one to fit."

They moved the ladders under the opening and came back to secure a new piece of drywall. Next, they placed another sheet to a set of sawhorses and Jessica handed him the tape measure. "Would you double check the size?"

"Didn't you just measure it, twice?"

"Dad always said measure twice, mark it, measure again, then cut."

Jeff laughed and headed back into the kitchen.

When he returned, she made neat marks and used the square to line them up before she grabbed a utility knife and scored it. They snapped it at the cut, and she sliced the paper on the back. A quick rub with a rasp cleaned up the few rough edges.

Jeff took the slender strip as it fell away when a man in paint splattered khakis and a light blue T-shirt entered the garage from the house. "Well, you're coming right along." Jeff recognized the dark-bearded man from the stage. He played the guitar.

"I've got some help." Jessica pointed to Jeff.

"I'm just the workhorse, Jessica is doing all the skilled labor."

She jerked upright and her mouth gaped open.

"I know, she's amazing." The man reached out a dusty hand. "David."

"Jeff."

"Right, I've seen you a couple of times with Jessica. Thanks for coming today. We can use the help."

Again, he pushed aside his fears. Jeff winked and leaned closer to the tall, solid man. "Happy to help, but I really came to hang with her for a while."

Jessica's face flushed as she rocked back on her heels.

David thumped Jeff's shoulder. "Can't fault you there, she's a good one. Wife talks all the time about how much Jessica donates her time. Always willing to help." David nodded at her as he continued through the garage out to his pickup at the end of the drive.

"I … We…"

"Come on, let's see how truly awesome you are and put this in the hole. I predict it will be a perfect fit."

"Well, be prepared to be disappointed."

As Jeff had promised, it fit perfect. Jessica disappeared for a moment and returned with ice-cold water bottles. They leaned against the framing of the sliding door and took long, deep drafts.

"You should take off the hoodie, you'll suffer heat stroke."

Jeff shook his head and changed the subject. "You know, I'm getting the serious impression you didn't need my help at all the day we met."

Jessica looked at her white-dusted sneakers. He doubted she'd respond. But her jaw clinched and her free hand fisted as her arm straightened. She muttered something he couldn't understand. She met his gaze directly. "In truth I didn't know the name of the fog boggers."

Jeff fought the smile tugging at his lips at her incorrect naming of the barb on foggers, but didn't interrupt.

"But I knew they were sprinkler parts and what a float arm is."

"Looks like you showed pity on me and let me pretend to help." Jeff's gut wrenched as the fears he'd been suppressing all day hit him like a tsunami. This had been such a bad idea. All of it. Letting her help him, helping her, going to church—

She cut into his thoughts as she continued. Her cheeks pinked, but her gaze never dropped from his. "You have no idea how amazing I found it to have someone else take charge. To not have to be the one who knew it all and takes care of everything. To have someone else *want* to help. You made my day—heck, *my* decade. For one brief moment in time, someone else cared enough to see to the problem and do something while I sat back and followed." Her words dripped with the same painful loneliness marring Jeff's life.

She opened up to him for the first time. In those few moments, she was more vulnerable than in any other day they'd spent together.

Her toe twisted and her shoulder shrugged. "You also got me headed in the right direction. They'd revamped the layout of the store since I'd last been in. I'd turned to where the plumbing used to be. But you knew where to go." Their gazes met again. "Thank you for caring enough to see me and help."

"You're welcome." The words were automatic and rote, but he meant them. What a unique woman. A rare lily in a world of carnations. *Please, let there be a way for this to last a little longer.*

Chapter 12

They were up and down the two freestanding ladders as they completed the ceiling before moving to the walls, Jessica and Jeff hoisted the sheets of drywall up and screwed them to the rafters. Almost every time they descended, she would grab waters and insist he take off the hoodie.

She amazed him. Nothing stood in her way or stopped her. She stepped to each challenge, considered it, and solved it all in the time Jeff took to register a problem existed. He found himself staring at her.

Jessica caught him several times. She ducked her head, a light blush kissed her cheeks. Twice, she absently tucked a stray wisp of hair behind her ear.

After fixing a second full row of drywall to the ceiling, Jessica put her fist on her hips. It drew his gaze to her figure, curvy, without being too skinny or overweight. "You have got to lose the hoodie. Jeff, you're already soaked through with sweat and it is only going to get hotter. Honestly, you can't drink enough to overcome the moisture you're losing. I don't want to have to drive you to urgent care, or worse, call an ambulance."

"I'll be fine. It's not—"

She snatched his gloved hand. The continued foreignness of the sensation of holding another's hand, especially hers, sent electricity firing through his entire body. How he wanted their relationship to grow. Jessica had become incredibly important to him in a short amount of time. Thoughts of her were beginning to consume him.

She pulled him across the backyard where a bright flowerbed sat enclosed by a retaining wall at the rear of the property. She sat on the stones and drew him down beside her before she relinquished his hand. "Okay, spill."

He stared at the black leather covering his tingling fingers with a profound sense of loss. "What?"

"Shame over your scars is keeping you hidden inside a hoodie. Tell me how it happened."

Jeff's heart stuttered and threatened to seize completely. "I … I can't." The words stumbled and caught in his throat.

Her voice softened. "Satan loves secrets. He thrives on them. We weren't meant for guilt and shame. God has set us free, but Satan doesn't want us to realize the chains we think still bind us, have already been broken."

Every part of him shook. He couldn't breathe. The end arrived before he thought. He' enjoyed their time together, but now his past hurtled at him to ruin everything.

Jessica stood with a small sigh. "I can't let you push yourself to heatstroke. Thanks for coming today. I hope I'll see you tomorrow." Melancholy dripped between them. She turned to leave.

She'd destroyed everything. What made her so inept? *Be bold.* That brilliant move compelled her to ask a man she barely knew to confess his darkest secret. Jeff had lost what little color he had left after working all morning in the oppressive heat in his heavy hoodie.

Jeff came today to spend time with me, and I forced him to tell me his darkest secrets. It is absolutely none of my business. It's not like I'm sharing my private information with him. Once again, I have gone and run off another person who could have been a good friend—I don't dare hope for something more.

The first two fingers of Jeff's gloved hand caught hold of her pinky and ring finger as she moved away. "Wait. Please." His anguished words broke her heart.

"I'm sorry. I should never have said anything," she whispered.

Jeff fought for breath as he clung to two of Jessica's fingers like they were a lifeline as he sank into the quicksand of his nightmares. The pull of the pit—heavy, gritty, and dark—tugged at his soul. "I don't want to lose you," he finally admitted. How, in four times together, had she become this important to him? Could he attribute his feeling to more than being lonely? Jessica was something special. He dared to glance up at her.

"Like not seeing me again will be any great loss." She rolled her eyes and her lips twisted in a dismissive smirk.

"You have no idea how your absence would hurt. Like you said, it's powerful when someone sees you and wants to help."

She didn't pull away, which continued to surprise him. She shook her head. "We have talked exactly four times prior to today. In the decades we have both been alive, our few meetings don't amount to a drop in the vast lake of time. You'd never miss me and my inappropriate nosiness."

He couldn't imagine tomorrow without her. "I would miss you deeply, Jessica. But if you knew what caused these scars, you'd have nothing to do with me, and I don't think I would survive your rejection. But, you just can't forgive me."

She held his fingers, gave them a little squeeze, and sat beside him again. Her soft, soothing voice comforted him with kindness. "It's not my place to forgive. God has paid for whatever you did. He did it thousands of years ago. All you have to do is accept it."

"You'd never want to be around me," he repeated.

She bit at her lip and squirmed beside him. "You don't have to tell me. I don't care what happened in the past. We have all done things in our lives we are not proud of and would rather forget." She rubbed her thigh. "We seem unable to put the past behind us, but God promises He does if we accept His gift."

Jeff sat still, clinging to her slender fingers. His head hung, swinging back and forth.

"Tell me or not, it's up to you, but I promise I won't look at you any different."

He knew what he'd done, and he learned enough of Jessica to assure himself she couldn't keep her promise. "You couldn't help it."

"What, did you murder someone?"

A jolt went through Jeff and he jerked upright. He released her fingers, but she didn't let go as he pulled a little from her and stared into her searching gaze. "No!"

"Then I'm confident my opinion won't change."

Jeff's head hung again. Like a free diver drawing in his last breath before descending, he pulled as much air into his taut lungs as he could. Better to get it out there. He could no longer ignore the woolly mammoth now exposed and about to trample his hopes.

Chapter 13

It took Jeff a few stuttered breaths before he could begin. "On a night in early September eighteen years ago, I'd been fighting with my wife, Molly. I stormed out of the house and went to a local bar to drench my wrath in a pitcher." The words eked out of him. Jeff needed to rip the bandage off this old wound and expose the rotting flesh, and then Jessica would know the truth about him. But the story dripped out like sap. Though she promised otherwise, Jeff believed this would be their final moments together and, as crazy as it sounded, he wanted them to last.

Jessica sat silently beside him. Her knee brushed his, and she still gripped his two fingers.

He could feel her intense gaze, but he refused to look up and meet it. "One pitcher turned into another. There might have been a third. I was livid—though now I don't even remember the argument." He dragged in a breath as a small shiver snaked through his body and grew to a full shudder. "Anyway, I stumbled out to the car and drove home. I hit another car almost head on and pushed it off the road into a field of tall grass." A deep quake ripped through him and his voice grew ragged. The memory gripped him hard and Jessica's presence faded.

"The car horn blared in the other vehicle as I slammed my shoulder against my door and forced it open. A woman slumped against the wheel. No one drove passed us, no cell phones back then, no houses nearby. I tried to open her door, but the fender had smashed against the door on the impact. She didn't move. I put my foot on the backdoor for leverage, I wrenched until I strained my shoulder." Jeff rubbed the joint as the memory brushed his muscle.

"With a groan, the door cracked open. Smoke stung my nose and bit at my throat. The hot underside of the car had set the dry grass on fire. The far side of the car started to glow as the flames grew." He coughed as a reflex like the smoke still rolled. "I got my body into the crack and forced the door all the way open. I had to get her out. But I knew you aren't supposed to move someone because it could caused more damage. But the glow of the flames continued to grow.

"She moaned as I carefully laid her on the ground. She mumbled something. I didn't understand her at first. Then I wished I hadn't. 'My baby.' At the moment I understood, a terrified wail came from the backseat.

"The flames were hot. The foul smell of burning rubber choked." He coughed again. "The fire had already blackened the window next to a tiny boy in his car seat. I took off my shirt and covered him as I fumbled with the car seat buckles. The heat grew unbearable. The baby went quiet. The latches on his car seat were jammed. I finally got the car's seatbelt undone and moved to take the whole car seat out with the kid in it. He shrieked! My shirt had caught fire. I threw it off and jerked him from the car." Jeff's stomach tightened into the familiar knot he knew always came before he vomited.

"Sirens filled the air. The flashing lights competed with the growing flames now consuming half the car. I know emergency people were all around us. But all I could see—can still see—is the red blistering welt on the boy's tiny hand. I didn't realize until I staggered back and fell the burns I'd suffered to my body. But I didn't care. I refused treatment, begged them to help the baby and his mom first.

"The next thing I remember, I was lying in a speeding ambulance. I had several surgeries to put grafts on the deepest of my wounds. Molly came by once but wouldn't stay as her nose wrinkled and her face went gray."

Jeff sagged, surprised he hadn't lost his breakfast. The old pain up his arm faded and any strength he'd possessed earlier in the day leaked out of him, and he wilted as he finished. But Jessica still hadn't left, so he told her what came next. "I didn't fight my punishment, pleaded guilty at the first opportunity. I couldn't get the boy out of my mind. After my time in the jail's infirmary, I spent a year in lock up. Molly served me with divorce papers. When I got out, I couldn't find her or my girls." Tears strangled his words. "I haven't seen them since."

The pressure increased on his fingers, and he again found himself on the retaining wall. Jessica clung to him as she remained beside him. She wiped a tear from her cheek, but said nothing.

Jeff couldn't breathe. He expected her to leave, or scream, or slap him, or do something.

Jessica looked out across the lawn to the house, still holding his hand. "How many times?"

Her gentle question came with no accusation. Neither did he expect. Not her query and definitely not any form of kindness. "How many?"

"How many times have you driven under the influence?"

Jeff stared at her. His answer emphatic. "Only the once. I never did it again. The smell of alcohol makes me ill."

Now she turned and considered him. Her brows pinched together and her head tipped. Her words were soft. "Okay, let me get this straight. You caused a car accident. But you also saved the two people in the other car. Then you accepted your consequences and suffered even more. Yet, even though you never did it again, you continue to hide in a hoodie?"

Jeff tried to pull from her hold. Why couldn't she understand the depth of his pain at the horrible thing he'd done? "I hurt a kid," he said with a groan wrenched up from his toes.

She shook her head. "You sinned. You repented—never did it again. I wish all of us could get it through our thick skulls as easily. We return to our sin again and again like a dog to his puke." She rubbed her thigh once more. "And I assume you've asked God to forgive you?"

"I try every day."

"Then why are you hiding?"

Why couldn't she understand? It had nothing to do with 'sin.' He had forever changed two lives. He wanted to alter the past and fix the consequences of his mistakes. Time travel didn't exist. "I am ... I ..." Jeff stared at her. What did she mean? Why couldn't she see?

Then as he expected, Jessica relinquished his hand, her head shook. But she remained at his side. She pushed up his sleeve, seized his scarred wrist and started to yank off his glove, finger by finger. "Jeff, Satan has your number!"

He should have closed his hand, stopped her. Her actions stunned him to immobility.

At last, she jerked the glove off and flung it to the ground. Then she did something he never could have dreamed. She slid her hand under his and laced their fingers together. They rested on his knee, and she pointed to the smooth waxy-looking scars patch-worked over his pale, pruney skin. "These are not your shame."

Chapter 14

The world had tipped off its axis. Or now spun in reverse. Or perhaps he found himself in an unbelievable dream. Jeff struggled to get a grip on the current events. Jessica asked him about his scars and—for no reason he could think of—he'd told her everything. But she hadn't run. Or struck him. No. Jessica sat beside him and held his hand. This flesh hadn't experienced the touch of another human in eighteen years. Their fingers were entwined and rested on his leg.

Jessica pointed to his scars with her other hand and spoke with earnest words. "These are not your shame. These are your honor. Yes, of course you sinned. You shouldn't have drank too much. Completely inappropriate to get behind the wheel while drunk. There is no question you blew it there. But it didn't end *there*.

"You had an accident. You never intentionally set out to hurt anyone, but it happened. In one moment, everything changed. You made a choice. A decision to make sure no one else would be affected by your wrong actions. You didn't run. At a significant cost to you, you got them both out of the car. These scars prove your honor, you take responsibility for your actions. It is clear; others matter more than yourself."

Her grip tightened on his. "Now, unmask yourself, *hero*."

Jeff jerked and stared at her. He heard her words. Comprehended them. But they didn't make sense. She couldn't have said he had been a hero in his horror story. "I'm no hero."

"You're right. Not for the accident, and definitely not for the DUI. It's stupid and criminal to drive drunk—wrong on many levels. But you are for what you did next. You rescued them, and didn't let them die, and those actions were right and brave and good." She jerked on his sleeve and pointed to the zipper of his hoodie. "No more disguises." She tugged on him again. "And so help me, if you have a long-sleeve t-shirt on under the sweatshirt, I will Gibbs-slap you."

He couldn't help the bubble of laughter that snapped the tension warring in him at her reference to a popular TV crime series where the boss lovingly smacked his people on the back of the head when they did something stupid.

Jeff reached to unzip the sweatshirt. She released his hand and jerked off a sleeve freeing him. When he slid out is other arm, she wadded up the shroud and threw it toward the dumpster they'd been using for the rebuild. It missed, but she didn't seem to notice.

Her finger skimmed down his arm. The sensation over his unfeeling grafts to his sensitive skin and back, tickled and sparked something in him. "These aren't bad. They are a badge of a brave, brave man." Their gazes met. A gentle smile turned her soft lips.

Jeff wanted to hug her. His heart rate increased. Her fingers locked with his again.

"No more hiding. No more shame. If you asked for it, God has forgiven you. Your debt has been paid in this life and in eternity if you've accepted it." She turned toward the house and then looked down at her feet with a sigh. "I'm afraid I lied earlier."

Jeff held his breath, his heart once again stumbled.

"My view of you has change now."

He lessened his grip on her hand, knowing she would leave now. The hope she'd raised against all odds, shattered on the jagged shards of his broken heart.

She squeezed his hand tighter. "I respect you even more now."

What? Jeff's thoughts and emotions suffered whiplash. *More? She had admired me before and now it's grown?*

"There you two are," Dave said as he strolled across the yard.

Jessica stood and her hand pulled from his. Jeff rose on quaking legs. She averted her gaze and bright pink flushed her cheeks. She reminded Jeff of a teen caught making out in her bedroom when her mom walks in. "We needed a cool break."

"Between the weather and the work, we're all frying like eggs in a skillet," David agreed. If he thought anything of them holding hands with their heads bent together, Jeff couldn't read it on David's face. "Well, I got my hands on a generator and some fans. It should be a least bearable if you're game to continue."

Jessica moved toward the house. "Of course."

Jeff followed in her wake. "Thank you."

David slapped him on the shoulder as he walked beside them. "Glad you're willing to stay and out of the sweatshirt. You gave me heatstroke to look at you." David continued on in a different direction as Jessica returned to the stack of drywall again.

Jeff took the other end without a word and stared at her smiling face. Jessica really was something else, and—heaven help him—he was falling in love with her.

Their connection had changed while they sat on the retaining wall. As they worked, Jessica smiled and talked as though they had been friends for years. "You've traveled a lot," Jeff said as she passed him the drill.

"I enjoy seeing other places. They can be different and yet much the same."

Jeff reached for the next screw to drive in, but he found the cup on his ladder empty.

Jessica descended her ladder and grabbed the container. "Run out again?" She took it from him and stared, a mischievous smirk twisted her lips.

"What's that for?"

"You remind me of Atlas."

"An atlas?"

She laughed, the soft chuckle he loved. "No. Atlas, the Greek god forced to hold up the world."

Jeff looked up as he braced his end of the drywall over his head to prevent it from snapping in half. "You intend to leave me standing like this?"

She shrugged and feigned searching for the bucket of screws. "Well, not forever. Only until I find …"

Jeff couldn't keep from laughing. The woman had more dimensions than he'd realized when she'd helped him with his load of plywood. Playful and thoughtful. A strong helper yet vulnerable. "We left them—"

She put her hand up to silence him. "No, no, don't tell me. I'll find them. Eventually." She shot him another cheeky grin.

"Preferably before all the blood runs out of my hands."

She shrugged again. "Let's hope."

Chapter 15

Jessica enjoyed a lunch break under the backyard trees, before she and Jeff finished hanging the drywall in the kitchen.

"You two are hired," David said as he inspected their work as the light began to fade on a long day. "I never dreamed we'd be this far along at this point. You two are quite a team."

"We are," Jeff said. Weight filled his words and again he stared at her. He'd looked her way a lot today. After she'd cornered him and made him spill his deepest darkest secret, he'd chosen to stay around. A horrified look had filled his face, and he quaked during the entire confession. Jessica believed he'd leave, and she'd never see him again.

But Jeff stayed. They'd talked and laughed, and she had almost forgotten the work they accomplished in the process. What made him hang around—and stare?

"I hope you can come back on the next workday," David said as he shook Jeff's now ungloved hand. Jeff stared at the hand a moment. David didn't seem to notice the fleeting glance. She remembered his story. He'd most likely hidden in a glove and long sleeves for almost two decades.

David gave her a quick hug before he turned to talk to the others still there. "See you two tomorrow?" he called.

"We'll be there," Jeff answered for her.

As they walked through the garage and down the drive, Jessica stood in a cool bit of shade and savored the growing delta breeze. The oppressive heat had finally snapped. She pulled her phone from her back pocket and opened the contacts. She entered 'Jeff Tate' in the name field and moved the cursor to the spot for the number and handed it to him.

"You asking for my number?"

Heat once again filled her cheeks. Gosh, she'd blushed a lot today. Her breath caught and she stared at her toes.

Jeff bumped his shoulder against hers. "You beat me to it." He handed her back the phone. She saved the information, clicked the camera app, snapped a picture of him, and added it to the contact she'd created. Then she opened another app but paused as her nail tapped on the screen.

"Do I get your number too?"

She shrugged and smirked.

"What are you doing?"

She glanced at him. "You need just the right ring tone. I thought about the sexy tractor song, but you're not a farmer." She tapped the screen again to stare at the music app.

"Sexy?"

She ignored him as a song came to her. "Got it." After she downloaded the tune, she set it as his ringtone, then hit play and the late eighties song 'Holding Out for a Hero' filled the early evening air. Jessica grinned at him.

"Seriously?"

"It's perfect," she assured him.

He shook his head a bit dubiously. "Do I get your number?" he asked again.

She texted him a grinning emoji.

His phone dinged, and he focused on it for a moment.

When he raised it to snap her picture, she covered it with her hand and turned away. "Don't you dare."

"You took *my* picture."

"You're a guy. All men can look even better after a hard day's work. I'm a horrid mess. Covered in drywall, sweaty, no make-up, hair's hideous. I'll break your phone."

Jeff lowered the device and his gaze narrowed on her. "We need to come to an agreement. I don't like how you talk about yourself. I wouldn't stand for anyone else talking to you the way you do. Here's the deal: every time you put yourself down, I put my hoodie back on."

She stared at him.

"You're beautiful. Inside and out." His fingers brushed her arm and goosebumps rose across her skin. "Are we agreed." He didn't say it as a question but a statement.

She offered him a single, slow nod.

"Good." He turned back to his phone. "I'll wait until tomorrow to snap your picture to give you a little time to adjust and accept the idea you have nothing to worry about, but I'd rather have it now." A tune emanated from his phone. 'You are My Sunshine.'

The lyrics hit her and caught on one word. "Love?"

Jeff paused before he gave a single nod.

She blushed again. Nothing made sense. Four lunches and one smoothie, and he picked a song indicating he loved her as her ringtone. She fought for an even step and a full breath.

He held open her car door. "See you tomorrow?"

She nodded as her emotions rolled and the world tipped uncomfortably.

Jeff jolted awake and coughed out the phantom smoke and rubbed the remembered searing pain from his arm. He sat bent over the side of his bed, his other arm pressed against his stomach. His cell phone lit up and dinged at the incoming message. He looked at the time. 2:37. Who would text him at this hour?

He tried to push away the flashback as he pulled the phone close and unlocked it. Jessica's name shone back at him. He read her text.

"There is now no condemnation for those who are in Christ Jesus. Romans 8:1 God has paid the price. Satan has no power over you."

He stared at it unblinking. "How did you know I was awake?" he texted back.

"I didn't. God woke me with the message. Thought I'd share."

"Thanks."

The grinning emoji popped up.

The grip of his flashback vanished. His lids grew heavy. He smiled as laid he back and fell asleep. The grin remained in his dreams. Dreams of Jessica.

Chapter 16

Jessica wore a flowing yellow sundress with large, bright red flowers. The wide straps revealed her sun-kissed skin. Her hair shone like burnished bronze as it hung in springy curls. Make-up covered her face. Though still pretty, Jeff preferred the more natural version from yesterday. "Good morning."

"Morning," she smiled. "Love the shirt."

Jeff glanced down at the Hawaiian print. "Yeah, figured if the sweatshirt in June had caught everyone's attention, I could blend in now." He nodded toward her. "Your dress is perfect."

She spun around. "Thanks. I changed my outfit a half a dozen times this morning. Spent over an hour on my hair. And almost as long trying to make my face somewhat presentable."

Jeff swiveled on his heel and headed for his car.

"Where are you going?"

"To get my hoodie."

She ran after him and stood in his path. "No, don't. I'm sorry."

Jeff looked at her. What made her constantly negative about herself? "We had an agreement."

"I know." She bit her lower lip. "It's a habit I've had for years. You can't expect me to end it overnight. Come on, let's go in before we're late."

Jeff let his left hand brush against hers hoping he could hold it. She pulled away and flashed a wicked smile. She twirled around behind him and came to his right side. Her fingers skimmed his palm and slid between his before they tightened. Okay, he'd forgive her the earlier slip about making herself look good enough to go out. He found her perfect in every other way.

David glanced at Jeff and nodded before the music began. As always, Jeff's mind wandered. He caught bits of songs about the love and forgiveness of God, but his thoughts were elsewhere.

No shortage of beautiful women gathered around him. Brunettes and blonds, Asian, Hispanic, African-American and mixes. He once again had missed most of the music and announcements as his own thoughts consumed him. He turned back and considered Jessica as they sat and the message began—his mind remained too distracted with wonderment of her to attend to the details of the service.

Jessica stood a couple inches shorter than him, and he wasn't a tall guy at five-seven. He liked the way the sun caught the gold in her hair, but the cut and style didn't stand out. She had a figure, but she'd never be mistaken for a model. Yet something continued to draw him to her. Something more than looks or physical attraction. She answered a need in his soul. She saw him when no one else wanted to, and she gave of herself. Jessica's beauty came from the inside.

She elbowed him and slid her bulletin onto his knee. Her feminine script adorned the edge. *You're staring and it's distracting.*

Jeff's gaze rose from the admonishment to her smirking grin and pink cheeks—though the blush hid under her heavy makeup. He preferred her construction look from yesterday. She took the next sermon note, and he tried to turn his attention to Pastor Matt.

Jeff had been to church as a child. Sometime during high school he'd stopped going. He never gotten much out of the fiery preacher other than to know of his coming damnation for being a sinner. After the birth of his first daughter, he and Molly had gone most every Easter and Christmas. But Jessica's church didn't resemble those services at all.

The pastor read from the Bible, and after another quick glance around, Jeff noted almost everyone had their own Bibles, or at least an app on their phone, open to follow along. From those he'd met, it seemed these people didn't go to church to make themselves feel better. They lived out what they learned, like Jessica had yesterday. She believed God could forgive him for the accident and hurting the kid and his mom, and thus she forgave him. If God wouldn't hold anything against him, neither would she.

She nudged him again. She gave a small lift of her chin toward Pastor Matt and Jeff tuned into his words.

"You heard me correctly, we are called friends of God. Yes, He is the all-powerful ruler of the universe, Creator of heaven and earth, but He walked each night in the garden with Adam and Eve. He wants the same intimate relationship with me and with you.

"Picture Christ on your sofa with his ankle up on his knee when you come in the door in the evening. 'Tell me about your day,' He says. 'I've been waiting to spend some time with you.' This is the God who calls us into relationship."

Jeff's mind tried to conjure up the image of the man he'd always seen in paintings sitting on his beat-up couch. He couldn't picture it, but the words wouldn't leave him. 'I've been waiting to spend time with you.'

Jessica dropped a check in the basket as she passed it, drawing him from his thoughts. He hadn't become a member, but Jeff had been attending regularly now. He should probably start giving some himself, but funds were a little lean at the moment.

After the final song, Jeff followed Jessica out and greeted Pastor Matt as they passed. "Hey," he brushed her arm as they walked toward the cars. "You willing to ride with me? I want to take you someplace new for lunch."

She hesitated for a moment before nodding and changed directions toward his truck. The gentle brush of her full skirt flapped against his leg as he took her hand.

Chapter 17

Jeff took her to Old Sac, the historic area of downtown Sacramento with its wood plank sidewalks and brick streets near the river. They'd had a pleasant lunch then wandered the lanes and checked out the quaint shops. Jeff held her hand as they moved from stop to stop before they turned and strolled beside the river.

Somehow it unsettled Jessica to be so at ease with Jeff. He listened and asked questions to draw her out, and she talked more than she ever had with anyone. He continued to share his struggles with his guilt after the accident. Jessica remained silent of her own shame. He seemed to like her, and she almost became ill at the thought of losing whatever they had growing between them.

"You know, it's odd when no one reacts to my scars," Jeff said, pulling her attention from her own conflicted musings and back to him again.

"With so much out there about wounded warriors and returning veterans, everyone probably thinks you are one."

He jerked to a stop. "Well, that explains it."

Jessica stared at him.

"I got gas before church this morning and the guy next to me nodded and said, 'Thanks for your service,' as he pulled out. I had no idea what he was talking about." He turned and smiled. "But brilliant you figure it out."

His phone buzzed in his pocket again.

"Aren't you going to answer? It's rung several times this afternoon."

"You can hear my phone? It's on vibrate. You continue to amaze me."

Jessica couldn't figure out why. "You don't intend to check the phone? You hiding a girlfriend or something?"

He squeezed her hand. "No, it's not her." He winked. "I know what she's doing right now."

Did he call her his girlfriend? Couldn't have. Heat flooded her cheeks again, and the air became heavy and hard to breathe though the day ended up much cooler from the strong breeze ruffling her hair. It had been something she wanted more than anything. Being in a relationship had been the one thing she cared, cried, and stressed about, for years. Then she'd given up. Now she didn't know what to think, but refused to hope.

She brushed a curl from her face. They were almost flat and Jeff still hadn't snapped her picture. She hated having her picture taken but if he intended to do it, she should at least look presentable. The longer he waited, the more her hair and makeup lost their best.

"I know who's calling. My website is being problematic again." He pulled her from her rambling thoughts once more. "A client is trying to upload some information for a job he wants me to do. I'll email him when I get home and get it what he needs."

Jessica pulled out her phone. "What's your site?"

Jeff rattled off the URL. "Why?"

She brought it up on her screen. There were a couple of pages with tons of writing on each, no real landing page and a few small shots of Jeff. The tab for the contact wouldn't open.

"By the wrinkle of your nose, I can see you're not impressed."

"I've seen worse." She had, but not by much.

"Know anyone who could help?"

She started to open her mouth, but clamped it closed and shook her head.

Jeff pulled them to a stop again. "What were you going to say?"

"It's nothing."

"Do I need to get my hoodie?"

She glanced up at him confused. She hadn't said anything—barely thought it.

"You have that look."

"What look?"

He moved in front of her and took both her hands in his. They were callused and strong, warm and reassuring. His gaze searched her. "Who do you know who can help with my website?"

"I used to do the site for the grant office."

"Good. Then you can help." He released one hand and pulled his phone from his back pocket. He tried to type with one hand but finally let go of her and used both to input some information.

"They hired someone who could do a better job," she said with a sigh.

"I trust you. Be honest—could you make it any worse?"

Her phone whistled an incoming text.

"Probably not," she admitted with a smirk.

Phone back in his pocket, he took her hand again. "I texted you my login and password. Have at it. I could use any help you can offer."

She intended to say, 'Don't set your hopes too high,' but snapped her mouth closed when he glanced at her with a raised brow. They walked and talk turned to different times they had each come to the river for various events.

Jessica pushed the nagging fear of the obscurities of their relationship aside and focused on his stories. The sound of his voice acted like a balm to her lonely spirit, and she could listen to him all day.

Chapter 18

After Jessica spent a few minutes with her fur-girls when she got home, she offered them a treat to keep them occupied and pulled out her laptop. She logged into Jeff's site and she took a closer look at what she could do with it.

After she fought with the hosting site for an hour, she closed his page entirely and started from scratch on a platform she knew well. She transferred his domain over and began to build.

The simple landing page contained a picture of him in a suit on one side, imposed over an office scene, while the other half showed a different shot of him in jeans and a long sleeved western plaid shirt with a horse. It would work best if from here, clients could then go to a single sight focused on either the office business or on the horse training.

She grabbed her phone and texted Jeff. "Do you have any other domain names than the one you gave me?"

"No. Do I need more?"

"Maybe?"

Jessica searched for some names to catch people's attention and stick in their memory. She settled on Tate Solutions for the office business and Hurting 2 Healthy Horses for the training. An H2H^2 in the form of a cattle brand could work for the logo of the second site. She contacted someone to design it, and she would develop an image for a logo of the office work side later.

Jessica glanced at the clock. Past seven and she only had the landing page done. Fear washed over her at the realization she'd taken down his site and while Jeff had maintained some form of presence on the web, now he had nothing. Jessica couldn't leave his current and future clients without access to him through the site.

She picked up her phone and dialed her manager. "Hi Vicki, it's Jessica, I'm sorry to disturb you at home."

"Hello Jessica, what can I do for you?"

"I'm going to take a personal day tomorrow."

"Okay. Is everything all right?"

"Yes, I just have a project for a friend I need to finish. I know I'm supposed to inform my direct supervisor, but …"

"True. But why can't you tell Kevin?"

Jessica told Vicki about the directive from Kevin to complete the report, and reminded her manager of the discussion which gave him the responsibility.

"Thank you, Jessica. I know you didn't want to tell me. I'll take care of this situation in the office tomorrow. When you return, we'll all have a sit down and iron out this situation."

"Thanks, Vicki. I appreciate it."

Jessica tried to breathe a sigh of relief, but she wanted people to like her. Her main goal in life continued to be geared to controlling every situation in order to cause others to think well of her. It seemed impossible, at this point, to make Kevin and Jeff both happy with her. Jeff stood as her priority at the moment, and she didn't give a flying fig what her lazy boss thought of her. Her attention turned back to Jeff's website and her need to make it the best. She wouldn't consider what would happen if she failed.

Jessica wrestled her fears aside yet again and called Healing With Hooves, the therapy stables Jeff gave his horses to. She startled when a person—not a voicemail message—answered. "Hello, may I speak to the owner, please?"

"This is Shannon."

"Hello. I'm sorry to bother you late on a Sunday evening. My name is Jessica and I'm—" A friend? Girlfriend? Acquaintance? "Jeff Tate has asked me to update his website. Could I come by tomorrow and take some pictures? These photos won't be of clients. I'm looking for some shots of the horses he has worked with where they serve now."

"Well—how about you come around ten? There aren't many clients scheduled then, and the ones who will be here should be fine with someone taking pictures."

"Thank you. Thank you very much. I appreciate this."

"Sure. See you tomorrow."

Jessica put the horse-training site aside and focused on his office business. She created a few pages including a secure one to share files which could only be seen if you were a client. She glanced at the clock. Almost 2 a.m. Time to turn out the lights, push the girls aside, and find a place in her own bed. But she couldn't go to sleep.

The excitement of creating something, helping someone, made ideas whirl in her head like frantic spinning tops. She should add this. Make sure to choose the right SEOs. Put an ad for Jeff's business on a site she knew to increase his traffic. But along with the exhilaration came the nerves. What if Jeff hated it? She'd paid for two new domain names. Sure, they were cheap, and she only secured them for one year, but …

Time to sleep. You can always worry in the morning.

Chapter 19

Her phone whistled in the living room where she always charged it. Jessica rolled over and looked at the clock. 7:30 a.m. The only texts she ever got this early were from Amazon, and she hadn't ordered anything in weeks.

A few minutes later it rang. She staggered to it, as she dodged her fleet-footed girls who were excited to be up. Jessica turned off the house alarm, let them out, and found her glasses to read the message.

Kevin: "Where are you? I need the report completed."

He also left her an intense voicemail. She messaged him back saying she talked to Vicki and wouldn't be in. She had to turn off her phone after the fifth text and forth call from him. Tomorrow would be nasty, but as she reviewed the previous night's work on Jeff's website, she smiled. Even she had to admit, she'd done a good job.

"Hello, I'm looking for Shannon." Jessica entered the stables and stopped the first person she came to leading a horse.

A woman called from behind her. "You must be Jessica. Welcome." Shannon stood a little taller than her and appeared to be in her mid-thirties. She wore her dark hair pulled up in a ponytail and had on shapely jeans tucked into knee-high riding boots and a polo shirt with the center's logo on it.

"Thank you again for letting me come."

"Jeff's a sweetheart. Love how he cares for the horses he brings us. I'm happy to return his many favors." She smiled and walked into the covered arena. "There is someone you should meet."

Shannon led her to an Asian woman standing beside a black horse with a boy about ten-years-old mounted on his back. His white helmet caught the light from the open side of the building. "This is Hwan, and her son Oliver."

"This is Midnight. I ride him." Oliver spoke in stilted, almost robotic words and he wouldn't look at Jessica as he pet the horse's mane. "I only ride Midnight."

"Hello," Hwan reached out her hand greeting Jessica. "Shannon said there would be someone here taking pictures today." With her name and looks Jessica had expected an accent, and it took her back a little when she didn't have one.

"I won't be taking any of you or Oliver. I just wanted a few—"

"We want you to take our picture and tell everyone about the great work Mr. Tate does."

"Oh!" Jessica startled at the mom's offer. "Okay. But I'll need a release."

"I'm happy to give you one."

"Shannon?" Jessica called after the retreating owner. "If I send an email here can we print it?"

"Sure." She gave Jessica the email address.

Jessica started scrolling through the apps on her phone. "I just have to find it."

"What do you need?" Shannon asked from where she now stood beside them.

"I created a release to use for my job a few years back. I'm pretty sure I did it at home. It should be in my cloud. I hope." After a few minutes of searching, she found it. Downloaded and emailed it. "I'll need to change the name on the top to Jeff's business and tweak a couple titles and update the names."

"Come to the office." Shannon led the way.

Jessica returned with the printed release a few minutes later and Hwan signed it. "Oliver loves coming here, but he struggled at first. He didn't speak much. He's autistic. The first time I brought him, he crouched down, covered his head, and rocked back and forth."

Jessica watched one of the trainers lead Midnight around with the boy in the saddle. Oliver cheered, threw back his head, and smiled large enough to look painful. And he talked—a lot. He gave directions to the trainer, jabbered to Midnight as though he would continue the conversation, and shouted to his mom to explain what he did on the horse.

"I didn't think I would be able to get him back to the car." Hwan went on. "Then Mr. Tate arrived with Midnight in a shiny trailer. Oliver loves anything on wheels. He'd never seen a horse trailer before. He walked over to it and touched it. Mr. Tate got out and seemed nervous. He wore the hood on his sweatshirt up and covered his hands with gloves. He looked at me and then Oliver and back at me. I told him Oliver liked different vehicles and offered to get him out of the way."

Hwan glanced at her son. "But Mr. Tate knelt beside my boy and told him all about the trailer. He showed him how it hooked to the pickup and how pushing on the brakes in the truck worked the lights in the back of the trailer. He showed Oliver all the different doors and windows and explained when to use each. Oliver opened the back with Mr. Tate's help and a big black horse's rump came into view."

She turned to Jessica and smiled. "I thought for sure, Oliver would curl up again, but Mr. Tate showed him how to unhook the lead and get the horse to back out. When Midnight stepped out, the big horse looked at Oliver, lowered his head, and rested his chin on Oliver's shoulder. Now you have to know, my son hates to be touched. Until he met Midnight and everything changed. Mr. Tate made all that happen."

It took Jessica a moment to realize she smiled almost as big as Oliver. It made her proud to know Jeff. Even as he ran from the world, he helped another overwhelmed by it. She snapped about twenty shots of Oliver and Midnight and later a few with his mom too.

She thanked them for their help and moved to get some generic pictures before she left.

"Excuse me."

Jessica turned to a man with a military haircut and a metal prosthetic right leg and arm.

"I'm sorry to intrude, but did I overhear you say you are collecting testimonials for Jeff Tate?"

"I came to take some shots of the horses he's trained for his website."

"Well, you can take mine too."

Jessica glanced to the office and Shannon caught her stare. She held up one finger and Shannon nodded.

Jessica turned back to the man. "Okay. Thanks."

While they waited for another release, he told his story. "My name is Arnie, but my friends call me Ringer."

She looked at him, and tried to figure out why.

"They teased me saying 'You're a dead *ringer* for the other Arnold— as in The Terminator," he added when she didn't seem to get it.

She laughed. "Oh, nice friends." He looked nothing like the actor, other than the android body parts.

"I was injured in my second tour in Afghanistan. I didn't want anything to do with people for the longest time. A friend from the VA told me about this place and I came because I knew I needed to get out or I would put a bullet in my brain. Jeff arrived about the same time to deliver the roan," Arnie pointed to a red horse outside in the corral. "He recommended Bell here, said she's affectionate and a good listener."

Arnie reached for the horse beside him and patted her neck. The mare turned and nuzzled against him. "It has been almost six years now. I work here and get other vets to come and heal with the horses. We couldn't do this without the horses Jeff trains."

Jessica took another round of pictures after Arnie signed his release. "Thank you very much for your time, your service,"—she shook his hand—"and your continued work with veterans."

"I wouldn't be here without Jeff."

Jessica smiled all the way back to her car. There were others who thought of Jeff as something special. She couldn't wait to put this information, and a few of her shots, up on his website to share him with the world. She wanted everyone to know about this hero.

Chapter 20

Jessica squinted against the glaring lights in her bathroom while she tried to pry her lids open enough to get her contacts in. She hated mornings, always had. This one started out particularly bad.

She'd finally finished Jeff's sites and hit "publish" after eleven—well, closer to midnight. She dropped in bed and tossed most of the next few hours until her alarm clock went off. *What if Jeff hates it? I should have had him look at it before I made it live. I gave him toll-free numbers, and powerful SEO search words, but what if …*

The endless list made her stagger around completely out of sorts. She fumbled with everything, as she got ready. She grabbed a protein mix, shaker bottle, and some fruit and hurried out the door. She forgot to tell the girls to be good in her haste. Thick traffic slugged along, more difficult than normal, as she headed to her office located on the outskirts of downtown. Everyone and their great uncle seemed to be moving in the same directions. *I should have taken it down before I left and had Jeff look at it.*

When she arrived and found her normal parking spot taken, she had to park on the far side of her level. Up a short set of stairs to the elevator, her mind swirled like a whirlpool in a water-recovery plant. *Could I log-on with my work computer and take it down?* She tossed her head as the lift dinged and the door cracked open. No, the company blocked most out-of-office host sites like the one she'd used to set up Jeff's pages. She'd have to wait until she got home and hope he didn't see it by then.

"Miss Easton, glad you could join us today. I need to speak with you."

Great, Kevin's attitude toward her had deteriorated to the point he resorted to using her last name. Again, she had hardly entered their office before he barked at her. She glanced at the clock. She had arrived on time—barely. "Let me drop my purse and bag, sir." She thought it best to mirror his formality. "I'll be right there."

"Do hurry. I have a lot of work to complete, as do you."

"Yes, sir." Before she could drop her purse in the drawer, her phone whistled an incoming message.

"That's harassment. We had training about it. You can't whistle at me. I'm not on display for you." Ian stood and shouted over his cubicle walls.

"I didn't whistle, Ian. It is a notification on my phone alerting me to a new text."

"You can't have your phone on at work."

"I'm silencing it now. The day's just started. Please forgive me and try to get back to your work, Ian. It won't be a problem again."

He yammered and couldn't get himself reined in as his mental issues raged out of control. "There are rules for a reason. We all have to follow them. No phones at work and no harassment."

Jessica sighed as he continued to lecture. "I'm sorry, Ian. I remember the training too. I'm turning my phone off now."

"Miss Easton, are you coming?" Kevin's tone suggested the answer better be yes.

"Yes, sir." She unlocked her phone to silence it.

She got a glimpse of Jeff's text before the preview window disappeared. "What did you do?"

Her empty stomach had twisted in knots and now it clenched tighter until she dropped to her chair. She managed to clock in for the day before she staggered to Kevin's office.

He stood behind his desk, arms crossed, a deep scowl pulled at his short beard. "Close the door."

It seemed like a pointless charade. Glass made up the entire front wall of his office, and closing the door wouldn't serve to hide them in here. Also, his office did not prove to be any more sound proof with the door closed than it did when it stood open. His shouted words were sure to be heard by all. Still, she did as he instructed and took a seat in front of his desk.

"I can't believe you pulled a stunt like this on me. We are supposed to be a team here, but you have failed to do your part. Have you decided you will no longer be a team player?"

Jessica barely registered his terse words. Her website design had made Jeff mad at her. He loathed what she'd done and now he hated her. She couldn't contact him until her break. Two hours—she would be in the throes of a raging anxiety attack long before then. She neared the breath stealing level now. *Please, Lord, let me make things right with Jeff. Please.*

"Miss Easton, are you listening to me?"

"I'm trying to figure out what stunt you think I pulled." She knew what he referred to but, at the moment, she didn't care.

His hands flew up and he roared. "Seriously!" Fists on his hips he took a wide stance and glared. "You knew I needed the report for the meeting yesterday. I told you to do it on Friday but you put it off and then called in sick leaving me hanging and open to reprimand. You had better have a doctor's note to justify your absence."

Something snapped inside Jessica. She wanted nothing more than to quit, storm out of his office, and fix whatever she'd broken with Jeff. But if she ended her employment, she'd be left with nothing. If she got Kevin to fire her—that would be a different matter. She might be able to sue for wrongful termination. Jessica's thoughts were beyond control. She'd never sue anyone.

She battled to regain the composure she desperately needed. When she spoke again, she didn't raise her voice. She resisted any tone of irritation and spoke as though she didn't have a care in the world. In truth, she had one—Jeff. "First, a doctor's note is not required by our office for a one-day absence. Second, I didn't call in sick, I took a personal day. Lastly, I made it abundantly clear on Friday when I left, I had no intention of doing *your* job."

Kevin slammed his fists on the desk. "You purposely took yesterday off to mess with me."

"I made the decision at the last minute. I didn't contact Vicki until after seven Sunday night."

"You can't take off time on a whim anytime you want. It constitutes an abuse of the system."

"As yesterday is the first day I have taken off since you started working here, how can it be considered abuse?"

Kevin stared at her. He dropped to his seat. The frantic clicking as he typed added to the growing throb in her skull. No doubt he looked up her leave requests. He wouldn't find any other than yesterday in the year and half he'd been working at the office. Jessica rarely got sick—on a workday anyway—and scheduled any appointments at the end of the day missing an hour at most. Even those instances were rare. His frown increased. No doubt, he could see the months of PTO time she had banked, while he took a couple of days off each month.

The volume came down when he continued. "Nevertheless, your responsibility is to contact *me* if you weren't coming in."

To be fair, she should have, but Vicki had advised against it. 'It's time for him to stand or fall on his own,' their manager had said. "I didn't want to hear how my need to take a day off would be tantamount to failing *you* for not doing *your* job."

He stood again and pointed. "Get out!"

"Are you firing me?" As always, she didn't dare hope.

His pointing finger dropped as knuckles of both hands thumped down on his desk. In a gorilla stance, he leaned forward on his stiff arms and glared at her, his red face beaded with sweat. "And do your job too? Not a chance."

She stood and returned to her desk. Her leg twitched as she tried to focus on the grant requests the other employees had cleared for her final approval. She rejected the first three on the first page. Why couldn't people follow simple directions? If you want thousands of dollars handed to you, doesn't it seem logical you would read over the requirements and complete everything to the letter? And if you are employed and trained to reject applications when they fail in these ways, wouldn't you do your job well to keep it?

Jessica didn't live in such a world anymore. People expected something for nothing and to stay employed no matter how they shirked their responsibilities to their employers. Jessica, on the other hand, came from the generation who still believed you served on jury duty and paid your taxes honestly. She considered citizenship a privilege, not a right to all, and everyone gave their best, not just enough to get by.

She glanced at the time on her computer. 8:31. The rate of her bouncing knee increased. Her break would never get here. If she took one now instead of at the 'approved' time, Kevin would be angrier with her. Did she care anymore? She needed to contact Jeff and fix whatever he didn't like. She could put up the old site if he wanted and kill all she had done. 8:33. *Lord, please.*

"Miss Easton, I need your assistance if you can be bothered to *help* me."

"Coming."

Chapter 21

Jessica had been right. A fierce anxiety attack gripped her before Kevin released her—yet break still hadn't arrived. Her imaginary elephant sat squarely on her chest, and she couldn't pull in a deep breath. Thoughts rattled around her head. It seemed like an entire week passed while she waited. At 10:00:15 she stood, snatched her phone, and all but sprinted to the elevator. She had Jeff's contact up before the doors opened on the first access to the parking garage. She moved to the outer edge to assure reception in the huge cement structure and connected the call.

She barely allowed Jeff to say 'Hey,' before she blurted a long stream of rushed words. "I'm sorry, I can fix it, I'll take it down as soon as I get home, I should have asked, I'm sorry, please forgive me—"

"Jessica!" Jeff broke into her plea. "Calm down. What's the matter?" His kind tone soothed her.

"You asked me what I'd done. You hate the website, I'm sorry."

"Jessica, stop." He sighed with a small chuckle. "What I hate, is text messages. You miss the tone of the words on a cold screen.

"You see, I got a call at five a.m. from a couple in New Jersey who have a traumatized horse they love. They want to bring him all the way to me to rehabilitate. Jess, you won't believe what they have offered to pay me. Before I could figure out how they learned about me in New Jersey, I got another call from So Cal with a horse donation for Shannon's place. He'll be here Saturday night.

"I opened my email then and I had seven new messages waiting.

One more about a horse, four wanted to hire me for accounting work, and the rest wanted to consult with me about small office networking and secure cloud storage. *That's* when I texted you.

"Holy cow, Jess! I've had another call and a dozen more emails since then. I've been on the edge as I've tried to keep my head above water, but with your amazing website, I'll be deep in the black by the end of the month. How'd you do it? And where did I get eight-hundred numbers? Most important, how much do I owe you?"

Jessica fought to catch her breath. "Wait, you aren't mad? You like it?"

"Are you kidding? It's amazing—you're amazing. Shannon has already called me and wants me to ask how much you'll charge to make over the Healing With Hooves site."

"Oh, I'd be happy to do it," she said as air whooshed out of her lungs. "I'm relieved you like it."

"Like it? I *love* it. Jess. The care and thought you put into it is one of the many reasons I'm falling in love with you."

The ground dropped beneath Jessica and her knees gave out. She slumped to one of the steel cables that prevented her from toppling from the parking garage. "What?" The question strangled out of her constricted throat. The cars blurred and her head spun. She started to hyperventilate.

"Miss Easton!" The door from the small stairwell banged open and Kevin glared at her. "Your hours will be docked and a formal reprimand added to your file if you continue to abuse your break time."

She lumbered to a standing position as her legs wobbled. She held her phone in a death grip as it hung at her side. She glanced at her watch. "I have three minutes. I'll be back at my desk on time." *Besides,* she thought, *you can't dock me time for taking my breaks.*

"I've been looking for you. I need to speak to you—*now.*"

"Yes, sir."

She staggered forward and brought the phone to her ear again. "Talk to you later." She disconnected before Jeff could reply. But he'd already said more than she could handle.

Jeff relived what had happened. The words had blurted from his lips and the phone had gone silent. Then it remained that way.

When he texted later to check on her after she got off work, Jessica had responded, 'Fine'. Then she'd emailed him all the information to get into his websites and how to assign numbers and passwords to clients to allow them to log-on to the secured page and send him documents.

She'd thought of everything—including separating his two sites but keeping them linked in a way too. The work couldn't be more beautiful, and the testimonials had nearly brought him to tears. He had no idea people held those opinions about him. Jessica continued to amaze him in various new ways every day. Still, his heart ached to know she didn't seem to feel the same way about him.

Wednesday passed with no contact from her at all, and the darkness descended again into his isolated corner of the world. Oh, how he missed her.

Thursday his phone dinged. "Can you meet me at the shopping center in El Dorado Hills?"

A sigh of resignation passed his lips. She wouldn't break up with him in silence, or over a text. She'd meet him face to face to be kind, though El Dorado Hills seemed a bit far. Did they have enough of a relationship to break up?

One more time he'd get to see her. "Of course. Where?"

"The fountains between the shops and the movie theater?"

"I'll be there. What time?"

"6-ish?"

"I'll see you then." For the last time.

Chapter 22

Jeff finally spotted Jessica on the other side of the man-made water feature. Her arms were wrapped tight about her as she stared at the spouting fountains. He decided not to shout at her and hurried to the road to cross to her side. He inched up beside her. "Hey," he whispered.

She startled but continued to stare at the water. "Hey." Her voice rasped like when she'd asked him 'What' after he inadvertently confessed his feelings over the phone. She didn't say anything and Jeff avoided being let down easily—or at all.

"Did you mean what you said the other day?" She stood rigid and stared at the water.

Jeff turned to consider what had captivated her full attention. He knew what she referred to, but again he avoided the inevitable. "What did I say?"

"You know?"

"I said you designed an amazing site. I'm still getting new contacts by the way. Also, my existing clients love the members only features."

She ignored his praise. "About your feelings?"

"About the website?"

"No!" A defeated frustration tainted her sighed word.

"About how I'm completely falling in love with you?"

"Yes," she said with a whimper.

"It's true. I didn't expect it. Never thought I would be close to anyone again. Even if I did, I never dreamed it would happen this fast. But I am completely smitten with you."

"Oh."

"It's all right. I understand you don't feel the same way."

"No, you don't understand." She quieted for a while, but trembled though the evening remained warm even with a light breeze. She mumbled something.

"What?"

She didn't respond.

"You said the same thing when we worked in the Hansen's kitchen on Saturday. What is it?"

Now her voice quaked. "Be bold."

"Be bold?"

"David said when I spoke to him that day, it was the first time he'd ever heard me say anything. It got me thinking, before you arrived, if I acted bolder, spoke more, I might have more friends."

"I'm glad you're speaking your mind more. Bold looks good on you."

She snorted. "Sure. My choice to *be bold* led me to corner you in the yard and pry your deepest secrets out. A brilliant move."

Jeff turned and looked at her again. Her rigid frame shook with tension wound tight enough to snap like a taunt rubber band. "But Jessica, my life changed the moment I confessed those secrets to you. It has been the best event in my life—save the birth of my daughters. I wouldn't trade it for anything."

Again, she said nothing.

He stared back to the water. "How are you going to be bold this time?"

A long silence stretched between them, and he feared she wouldn't say anything. "I don't do hope."

"What?"

"I can't hope for anything. I've tried. I could hope for friends, but I don't have any. Or I could for employees who know their jobs and put in some effort, or a boss who does his own work and doesn't become a raging monster when I won't do it for him, hasn't worked. Hope leads to disappointment. If I don't hope then I avoid bouts of depression, I can be surprised when good comes my way, but I can't hope for …"

Jeff eased behind her and slid his arms around her waist. As he drew her close it felt like he held a marble statue in an earthquake. "Shh," he whispered in her ear. "Jess, you're starting to hyperventilate. Take a deep breath. It's going to be all right. Shh."

Her breathing calmed, but she remained stone.

"I'm terrified too. Nothing like this has ever happened to me."

She snorted again.

"Oh, I had crushes on girls in school, and I have been married. But I never felt this way with Molly. It has never been this deep or intense." He pressed a gentle kiss to her temple. "You are extra special, Jessica."

"You only believe what you feel with me is different because you've hidden yourself away for two decades. Now you're out in the world again, you'll see."

"I'll see what?"

"What every other man on the planet has seen. I'm not worth your time."

He tightened his arms around her. "Now Jess, not every man on the entire earth has rejected you."

"I can literally count the number of dates I've been on using one hand. Only two of those were *second* dates. I've tried the dating apps. No one even wants to talk with me, let alone go out."

He kissed her temple again. "Then I am the luckiest man around. I found the treasure everyone else missed. You're all mine."

"But for how long?"

"As long as you'll have me."

"I can't hope you'll stick around, trust your feelings won't change. I can't."

"Do you know how I do it? How I managed the fear of thinking you were coming here today to break up with me and say you never wanted to see me again?"

"I didn't plan—"

"I know, *now*, but when you didn't speak to me for two days, the fear took hold. But do you want to know how I survived it?"

She gave a small nod. The only movement she'd made, other than to talk, since he arrived.

"Each night after I turn out the lights, I'm grateful for the time I've spent with you. Whether we shared a meal, talked, or texted, my day had been brighter because you were a part of it. You are my sunshine, you know. My only sunshine."

Her lips curled in a small smirk he could just make out from where he stood behind her, and held her tight. She lowered her head a little as her cheeks pinked.

"Each morning I get up and wait. It will be a day like any other, unless you are a part of it. If you aren't, I cling to the memories of the days I have seen you, and the many times we talked and texted. Those times help me get through today without you. That's my secret. Today. I only have this day and my memories. Tomorrow, everything can change and you could leave my life, but today—today is a *good* day. Today, you opened up to me about your fears. Today, I got to hold you in my arms."

"Today," she murmured.

"Just today. No hope required."

A long breath eased out. "Today," she whispered again. Like an ice sculpture outside, her barriers melted. Her muscles relaxed and she leaned back into him. Molly had never snuggled. Even before his scars, she rarely showed physical affection in any fashion.

Jeff kissed Jessica's temple again and her head lulled back to rest on his shoulder. Her arms unwound, and her hands caressed his. "Today," she sighed.

"Is a *very good* day."

Chapter 23

Jeff still held Jessica tight in his arms. He loved the way she fit against him. "I don't *want* to move, but do you think we can go get something to eat? After your text, the thought of food only added to my nausea."

"I haven't been able to eat much either this week." She eased from his grasp and turned around. "I've been rather out of sorts." Again, a bashful smirk pulled at her lips.

"Can I ask, why did you want to meet here? El Dorado Hills isn't anywhere near either of our places."

"The water fountain calms me down. Ocean waves, waterfalls, fountains, they're relaxing."

Jeff stifled a chuckle, "If this is you calm, I'd hate to see you stressed."

She slapped his arm playfully, "It's all your fault, you know. Be nice."

He laughed. "I'm not sorry I told you." With the fountain as a backdrop, he pulled his phone from his pocket.

"Now? You want my picture now? I'm in my work clothes. Most of my makeup is worn off. The wind also keeps blowing my hair in my face."

"Do you know how many professional model shoots rent expensive wind machines to get this wind-blown beauty?"

She started to open her mouth.

"Smile, or I'll take it with your lips gaping." He grinned as she turned at an angle, stuck her tongue out at him, and struck a pose. He loved her. What a crazy thought. Is this the feeling people described when they talked about falling in love at first sight? Jeff never believed such a thing possible, but he couldn't deny he had fallen for Jessica hard and fast.

"Would you like me to take a picture of you together?" A young blond woman with a stroller stood behind him.

"Yes, please. Thank you."

She offered him a sweet smile and took the phone. "Why don't you look at each other?" she said.

Jeff stared into Jessica's eyes. She searched his face. He wondered what she hoped to find. When he glanced up again, the woman had turned and walked away—with his phone. Jeff ran after her and stood in her path. "Wait … you forgot my phone."

"Get away from me or I'll scream, you creep."

"My phone." He took care not to touch her or the baby she had slid his device next to, but he didn't intend to let her leave either.

"So help me, I'll scream."

"Go ahead, I'm recording the whole thing," Jessica stood to the side of the thief, her phone in hand.

At that moment, a police car drove by. "Officer!" Jeff shouted as he waved him down while he still kept the woman from fleeing. "She stole my phone."

The tall cop pulled to a stop and stepped from his vehicle. The waning light reflected off his bald chocolate-colored head.

"He's following me. They both are. He won't leave me alone," the woman lied.

Jessica approached the officer and held out her phone for him to see. "This is his contact." She poked the screen and "You are My Sunshine" played from beside the baby. "Clearly, she has his phone."

"Stop her! She took my phone." An ebony-skinned teen ran toward them. "She has my phone."

The officer squeezed the radio mic on his shoulder. "Yoshimi, I'm at the north end of parking lot three. I need assistance."

"On my way," filled the air followed by radio static.

A short officer pulled up a couple of minutes later and a slender olive-skinned man got out of the passenger's seat. "There she is. The woman who stole my wallet."

Bystanders milled closer to view the action.

"All right, miss, you are under arrest. Yosh, call CPS?" the first officer said.

The woman jerked back and pulled the stroller to the side. "No, you can't take my baby. You have no proof—"

The crowd around them thickened.

"It's obvious you have this guy's phone," the first officer pointed a thumb in Jeff's direction. "And with three more accusing you, there is ample probable cause."

"Don't touch me. I'll sue you. Police brutality!" The woman screamed, but Jessica and several others recorded it all. Neither officer had come near her yet.

Yoshimi got a hold of the side of the stroller and yanked. The action served to pull the baby from the thief's hands, and jerk her off balance in her high heels. The first officer turned her around and cuffed her. A blanket tumbled out of the stroller onto the sidewalk, and the gathered crowd inhaled a collective gasp.

Yoshimi gingerly turned the bundle and unwrapped a rag doll.

"If there is no baby, what's in the bag?" Jessica raised her chin to the large purse on the back of the stroller.

The first officer opened it up and scowled. "More wallets and phones."

The handcuffed thief kicked at the police and screamed obscenities.

The muttering in the crowd grew. "Thief! How low can you go? How could you pretend to have a baby? You're despicable!" The rants increased in volume.

"I'm not going to work for minimum wage," the woman spat.

"I did." Jessica said.

"So did I," echoed the first officer.

"Me too," added Yoshimi.

"I still do," Jeff said, and many others joined their cry.

Jessica stomped toward the woman. "You want it all without putting in the hard work we all did. Honest work is hard, and you want a hand out. You got a trophy for everything you ever tried, whether you won or failed and now you think the world owes you just for breathing."

The crowd cheered Jessica on.

"That's right."

"You tell her."

"Lazy, thief."

Jeff marveled at her. He had seen many different sides of her in the last hour. Her vulnerability in crippling fear, the tenderness of her affection, and now the strength in her call for justice and fairness. He continued to see more to love.

The woman screeched all manner of foul words as the sheriffs pulled up. After the reports were taken from all the victims and the videos from the crowd were sent to the officers, Yoshimi approached Jeff. "We'll need to keep the phone as evidence."

"You've got to be kidding," Jeff said with a groan. "It's the only contact I have with my clients. I'm self-employed. How long will you keep it?"

"Does that mean you're keeping mine too?" the kid asked.

"Give me a minute." Yoshimi put up one finger, turned, and spent a moment with the other officers on scene. He smiled as he returned. "This is what I need you to do, to allow me to return your phones here. We need to photograph them. I need you to look to see if she made any calls, accessed any sensitive data like a banking app, or if she downloaded anything."

Officer Yoshimi handed the kid his phone first, and they went through the process of searching it. When nothing different or new turned up, the officer had him sign a waiver and release and returned his phone.

Next the officer turned to Jeff, and they did the process all over again with his device.

"No new pictures, apps, messages. Nothing important has been opened. Only an app where I read the news."

"Those type of apps tend to stay open and don't allow the phone to go to sleep and lock," the officer said. "If you're sure it hasn't been tampered with, you can sign the waiver and release and have it back."

"The thief didn't have any time to do anything. I stopped her only feet away. Thankfully, the other officer drove by at that moment." Jeff signed the documents and received his phone.

The other officer worked with the man who had identified his wallet, and he got it back too. There were still five phones and three wallets left to return to their owners.

The crowd dispersed and Jeff's stomach growled. Yoshimi smiled and offered his hand first to Jessica then Jeff. "Sorry for your trouble." He shuffled his weight. "My wife told me yesterday we're expecting, and I kind of freaked when the *baby* tumbled out."

Jessica smiled. "Congratulations."

"Hey, before I go, you said you didn't get your picture together?"

"No."

The officer pointed toward the fountain now awash in lights with a deep pink sky behind it. "I'd be happy to, and I promise to return your phone." He winked. "It will be a picture of a day to remember."

"You don't know how much I want to remember this day." Jeff moved toward the water and wrapped one arm around Jess. She eased next to him and snuggled into his embrace. He turned and looked at her. "You're beautiful."

"You really need to get out more."

Yoshimi handed back the phone and waved his goodbye.

Jeff took Jessica's hand and turned her toward the many restaurants. "What I really need to do is go get my hoodie. You've been overly abusive this evening. I gave you some slack because you were under a lot of stress, but …"

"Can we just eat? I'll try to do better."

He slipped his arm around her again, and she pressed close. "What are you hungry for?"

"Food."

"Well, that isn't particularly helpful."

She smirked at him but wouldn't offer anything more. Oh, he truly loved this woman. And today she stood in his arms.

Chapter 24

Conversations fluttered around them. Laughter bubbled up from time to time. Wait staff wove among the tables. Everything around her said she sat in a typical restaurant on a normal night. But Jessica sat across from a man who'd professed to falling in love with her—twice. She never thought she'd hear those words. Stopped dreaming about it years ago. She despaired of ever having a friend the day they met. She still had no idea how to process his proclamation. But she couldn't deny the way he made her feel when he wrapped her in his arms. Could there be anything better than his warmth and strength surrounding her?

"Did I hear your boss yell at you over the phone the last time we talked?" His words were gruff.

"Yeah, I'm on his naughty list at the moment."

"I can't say I like the man."

Jessica cocked her head at him. "You don't even know Kevin."

"I didn't care for how he spoke to you. Molly always said I could be overly protective of the people I care about."

Jeff mentioning his ex-wife and his feelings for her in the same breath caused an odd whiplash to her rattled emotions. Again, she didn't know what to do with all the new sensations whirling around in her like an oversized load in an out-of-control drier.

As they ate, Jessica told him about the report Kevin had been assigned to create, his demand that she do it, and how her absence on Monday had left him in the spotlight alone.

"I'm sorry I made you miss work."

"You didn't make me do anything. The work on the sites excited me in a way my job hasn't in forever, and I couldn't stop. I had fun, more than I've had in—well, in years."

"The sites are great. I can't believe the response I've gotten already."

"The secret is SEOs."

"SE what's?"

"Search Engine Optimizers. The words you link with a site. You pick the most relevant words to allow your site to come up first when someone searches the Internet. They are then able to find you at the top of their search. Easy to remember phone numbers don't hurt either."

"I love the H2H^2 logo and 1-800-555-WHOA. How'd you come up with them?"

Jessica shrugged. "I have a weird brain."

Jeff stared at her.

"Weird isn't necessarily *bad*."

"Several of my clients are nervous at the prices on the site."

"You don't charge enough. If it makes you feel better, tell them they are grandfathered in at the previous rate, because they were smart enough to choose you in the beginning. Now you're in the big league, and everyone else will have to pay more."

"But don't you think it's a little high?"

"Minimum wage is currently eleven dollars an hour and working toward fifteen, right? And you have a very specialized skill. Shouldn't those two factors alone warrant at least fifteen to eighteen dollars?"

"Maybe."

They ate in silence for a while. "How will you deal with Kevin?" The way he spit the man's name out made Jessica take note never to let them in the same room together.

"Our manager, Vicki, called us into her office yesterday. Kevin thought I'd ratted him out to Vicki. She informed him the other staff had been upset with how he treated me and the general mood of the office. Vicki told him, he couldn't corner me alone anymore. She has to be there to mediate between us."

"I'm glad someone is looking out for you. Have you thought of quitting?"

"Every. Single. Day. But what else am I going to do? I'm too old to start over again. I still need insurance. I can't draw on retirement or Social Security anytime soon."

"Design websites," Jeff said as he took a big bite of steak and stared at her.

"I couldn't …" Could she? *Could I find enough commissions for website building to make a living at it?* The appeal of working for herself and from home almost proved to be too much for her hope-deprived heart.

"Of course you could. You're great at it. Several of my clients are interested in hiring you."

"I don't know the first thing about how to set up a business or figure out how much to charge."

"It's easy. I can help you with a DBA—Doing Business As license. The price should be easy to calculate because according to your logic, you should make at least minimum wage plus your skill."

"But I don't have any formal training."

"You have experience. How many websites have you looked at in your job?"

"Thousands."

"Experience. How long did it take you to do my sites?"

She focused on her plate.

"Mine proved to be such a mess, you had to start from scratch."

"Your platform stunk."

"Granted. Let's start over, excluding the time you wasted on the old site—when did you start?"

"Sunday, late afternoon."

They went back and forth with the times as he pulled each detail out of her. He grabbed his phone and did some calculations. "If you only charge minimum wage for your time, you're looking at about three-hundred and sixty. I'd say not less than four-hundred for each site."

Jessica nearly choked on her food. "Good grief! No one will pay those prices."

He still had his phone in his hand. He typed and set it aside. It dinged a minute later. He showed her the texts.

"Paul, my web designer says she'll charge a minimum of $400. What do you think?"

"I'm DEFINITLEY interested. Give me her number."

"See." He flashed her a smug smile.

Jessica got a box for her left overs as she almost always did and he, of course, paid.

"You know you wouldn't have been treading water with your finances if you let me pay once in a while."

"What kind of hero would I be if I let my girl pay?"

His girl. It sounded odd for many reasons. Yet, it made her heart flutter as it never had before.

He held her hand as they walked to her car. "How do you think it will go tomorrow?"

"About the same. We have our end of the month meeting on Monday. It's the one I have to produce a report for. Kevin has kept be too busy to complete it. We have a system to allow us to mirror any of the staff's computers on ours. With it, we can oversee what they're working on or check to see if they're playing solitaire or on social media."

"You think Kevin has mirrored your computer?"

"It would explain why every time I've tried to work on the report, he needs something from me, or wants me to help one of the staff. It's like he's distracting me with anything to keep me from completing it."

Jeff squeezed her hand. "Will you be able to finish it on time?"

She laughed. "Oh yeah. Done them for years. Have a template all set up. Drop in the latest figures in three columns and the spreadsheet does the rest. Under five minutes it can be done *and* printed."

He stopped next to her car and opened his arms. Jessica sprang into his embrace. It could have been the novelty of being with someone, or maybe everyone felt this way. Could she be in love? She'd never been remotely—what had Jeff said? Smitten. The word made her smile. She'd never been smitten before or had a crush. How did she know what she felt was love? But she knew one thing: she liked it and hated it at the same time. She never wanted it to end and didn't know how to make it last. But there hope sprang up again and tried to worm its way back into her life.

Today. She would enjoy whatever they had at this moment and be sure to thank God for it tonight. Tomorrow would be any other day. Probably.

Chapter 25

After he watched Jessica drive off, Jeff returned to his truck and scanned the pictures on his phone. Officer Yoshimi had snapped several. Jeff paused at the last one where they stared at one another. His arm wrapped around her, and the sunset caught in her hair turning the blond strands strawberry. For one instant, she stood open to his growing love. In the frozen moment on his screen, he couldn't see any fear. The officer had caught her believing—and hoping.

Jeff stopped on his way home and had a print made of the beautiful shot of them together and another smaller one of her sticking her tongue out. He didn't realize he'd taken it. The snarky little one he left in the visor of his truck and took the other inside. Once he emptied a frame of a picture of his first horse, he replaced it with the shot of his new love. He moved it several times until it landed on his bedside table. Now he'd see her first thing when he woke and last before he slept.

His phone dinged and flashed with her image. A jolt like lightening zapped through him. "Thanks for 'today,'" the text read.

"Thank you too." He added a heart emoji.

The next morning, his phone lit up again about 7:30. He'd started silencing it after a couple early east coast calls. He looked at the text. "Today," with the winking emoji.

For someone who didn't do hope, her behavior seemed hopeful. He gave her a thumb's up and "Today," in reply. He sent it and remembered she must be about to head to work. "Have a good day at the office."

"I'm not holding my breath," came her quick reply.

Almost six the next evening, Jessica dragged herself into the house as the girls yapped their welcome. Her phone whistled.

Jeff. "How'd it go?"

"As expected." She collected the girls' dishes and started to fill them when another text came in.

"Talked to David. He can't get a group back to the Hansen's for a couple of weeks. The next step is to mud the dry walls. It will take drying time in between each coat before we can painted. I offered to go over tomorrow and see what I could get done."

Jessica sat down the girls' bowls and poked the receiver icon. "Hey."

"Hey." His overly excited response made her straighten. They'd seen each other yesterday.

"Want company?" she asked.

"Always."

"Okay." His enthusiasm left her befuddled, but she marveled at the way it made her feel. She didn't like being out of control and whatever they had going on between them qualified as; riding bareback on a runaway horse, barreling over a cliff into a raging torrent of water, on the way to join a tsunami wave. She took a deep breath. "What time?"

"Are we talking now? Or tomorrow?"

"Ah …" She hadn't considered this evening. She wouldn't be opposed to seeing him—it simply hadn't crossed her mind. "Let's start with the Hansens."

"Let me call them and see if there is a time they'd prefer. Get back to you in a sec."

Jessica dropped on the couch. She thought she appreciated he had texted. She believed she enjoyed hearing his voice. Could she trust her feelings? Or the better question should be—what were her feelings?

Her phone whistled. "How about 9 a.m? Should not be as hot."

"Okay. See you there."

"I'll pick you up."

"You don't know where I live. I'm in South Sac. Their house is between us. It's out of your way to get me and then drop me off again. Meet you there."

"All right. What about tonight?"

Jessica stared at the message. Her heart did its weird flutter again at the thought of seeing him. But she didn't feel in the mood for another meal out. They always ate out, and it showed in the tightness of her clothes.

"Please." The next text came in with a crying emoji.

The girls were done eating and now jumped all over her. They'd be in a snit if she left again. She sighed and sent her reply.

Chapter 26

Jeff had eagerly put the address Jess texted him into the GPS app and changed his shirt. He headed to a neighborhood on the north side of Elk Grove. Hadn't she said she lived in the South area of Sacramento? He turned off the frontage road and drove a quarter of a mile next to the freeway until he came to a park enclosed by a chain-link fence. He pulled in behind her SUV. *So, not her house and not her neighborhood.*

She sat on a bench inside a double-gated entry. Jeff passed through the first gate and reached for the second when two Chihuahua mix dogs headed his way and barked. The black one came closer than the tan one but both their tails wagged at a fever pitch.

"Hush you two." Jessica stood and accepted his hug as the two dogs, he now realized were 'her girls' continued to raise a ruckus.

Jeff sat at the other end of the bench and tried to coax them over. "Hi there."

The tan one backed up and howled her disapproval.

"Sorry, she's not a fan of men."

"And how many has she met?" A jealous ripple shuddered through him which surprised him. The relationship between him and Jess didn't, in any way, resemble what he'd had with Molly, or any other woman he'd ever known.

"Only my dad and the other men we sometimes see around the park. She pretty much scolds each one the same way."

The black one inched up and sniffed his fingers before she gave them a lick. "Hi." He tried to pet her, but she scooted back.

"This black one is Licorice. Her name suits her. She licks—a lot. You'll be fast friends before we leave. The other one is Toffee. She'll probably never like you."

Jeff laughed. "Good to know." He turned and looked at Jessica. "I thought we planned to eat."

"I texted you to bring a beverage."

He held up his soda, and she started to pull items out of a reusable shopping bag. He soon had a plate with warm creamy pasta and a tomato and cucumber salad in his hand. "I don't think I have ever had a date at a dog park before."

She looked at him for a long moment then resumed filling her own plate. "Well, then it's a good thing this is a picnic with furry entertainment."

"They do tricks?"

She flashed him the smirk he loved. "Oh, sure. Licorice will beg, using her cuteness to convince you she needs everything on your plate. Then, if you aren't watching, Toffee will sneak up and steal what she would never take from your hand. They're a riot." Jess popped open a tub with watermelon slices and left it between them.

They ate for a few moments and watched the girls chase nothing and each other. They were actually quite entertaining.

"Did Kevin let you get your report done?"

"No. Kept me running all day. I'll have at least thirty minutes on Monday before the meeting. More than enough time."

Licorice came to a stop and sat up looking from Jeff to Jess.

"You've had your dinner. Go play," Jess waved her off, but she stayed and sat.

"Is she pouting?"

"That dog is the queen of puppy-dog looks. Don't let her fool you. She can put on a great act."

Jeff tried hard to ignore the little black dog, but the bit of white fur on her chin appeared to quiver as if she cried. Licorice moved to his side out of sight of Jess, and he slipped her a bite of pasta. She licked his fingers clean, and Toffee barked.

"Tattle-tail," Jeff muttered.

Jess laughed. "She won't take anything from you, but she hates the fact Licorice will."

They talked as a cool breeze eased the heat of the day away.

Jeff finished and put all the dishes back in her bag before he moved it and slid next to her. He put his arm around her and drew in a deep satisfied breath. Toffee yapped at him again. "You will have to learn to share." The little dog howled. Jeff kissed Jess on the cheek.

Jessica remained tight, rigid almost. But after a moment she again melted into him. She finished eating and the dogs finally ran off careening around the park at an impossible speed from animals with such short legs.

At last Jess rested her head against his shoulder and wove their fingers together. He could stay like this forever.

The dogs flew at the fence behind them snarled and bared their teeth. A big dog on the other side challenged back in an angry enough tone to make the hair on Jeff's arms stand on end.

He thought he heard Jess growl herself as she leapt to her feet and ran to the girls. She hooked the leashes to their harnesses as fast as she could while they squirmed and snarled. She got Toffee under her arm and reached for Licorice, as the inner gate opened with a nerve-grating whine to allow the Doberman entrance. The little black dog bolted from Jess straight at her larger, fiercer counterpart. Jess screamed and stomped on the leash. Jeff scooped up the agitated dog. Licorice didn't realize who had her as she snarled and fought to get at the newcomer.

The teen released the leash of the big dog and the fierce beast lunged at them. Jess turned, putting her back to the threat and shielded her little pet from the bared teeth.

Jeff stepped between them and caught the bigger dog by the scruff of the neck and held him at arm's length. Thankfully, the beast wasn't full-grown, though it out-weighed both Jess' dogs by three times. The skinny, black, monster was all legs with a mass of muscles in his core.

"What'd you think you're doing? Let him go. We have a right to share the dog park," the owner said.

"Sharing is caring," Jeff muttered first. "I'm saving you from being sued and your killer dog put down. Get your beast under control or I will. I can guarantee you won't like it if I have to do it." Jeff held tight while the youth waddled over. Despite red boxers reveled by his sagging shorts, he had an arrogant hitch to his stride.

Jess snatched their food bag and her purse and raced to the gate. She glanced back at him.

"Get your dogs in the car." Jeff nodded for her to continue.

"I think I'll let Wolf rip your throat out," the kid smirked.

"I'll snap his neck before he has the chance." Jeff lifted the snarling dog fully off the ground as he thrashed and gave the beast a shake. The sixty-pound mongrel writhed as he dangled with minimal strain on Jeff's arm. He was grateful for all his work with horses and the construction around his home.

Jess put Toffee and her bags in the car, returned, and reached for Licorice from outside of the fence.

It had been fortunate Jeff had scooped the little dog up while he stood close to the encloser. He kept his eyes on the kid, and a firm grip on the Doberman held as far to his right as he could, and passed Licorice to Jess. He knew he could toss the cur aside and hop out too before the dog could get him, but he waited until Jess had both her dogs safely in her SUV. He prepared to let the dog go when sirens screamed toward them. Help had arrived fast.

Chapter 27

Jessica stepped closer to her SUV as a sheriff's car pulled to a stop in the middle of the street. A fit officer in dark glasses with a military haircut jumped out.

"You all right?" he shouted to Jeff.

"At the moment," Jeff said.

Jess stood beside her car shaking as Jeff fought to keep the vicious dog under control. She marveled at his strength while she berated herself. Distracted by Jeff and his embrace, she'd let her guard down and hadn't noticed the troublemaker coming. She always watched for this dog in particular. He'd almost taken Licorice's head off the first time they met, and the Doberman had been a puppy a little bigger than her dogs at the time. The punk who owned the attacker had laughed. From then on, Jessica had always watched for them and left long before they neared the park. But this evening her attention had been elsewhere, and Jeff could end up paying for it.

The officer popped his trunk and took out two poles like animal catchers use. He entered the dog park and secured the hoop on the end of each pole around the dog's neck before Jeff released the killer. The kid shouted at the officer to let his dog go.

A second, plumper, deputy arrived and Jessica moved to stand outside the fence.

"Who owns the dog?" the first officer said.

"I do." The kid popped his chin up toward Jeff. "And I wanna file charges against him for attacking Wolf."

The second deputy took one of the poles. With all four paws on the ground, the beast proved to be stronger and more agile than when Jeff had him dangling in the air. The officers struggled to keep the dog in check. Wolf snarled, jerked, and lunged.

Jessica shuddered and folded her arms tight. She blinked as she realized she wanted Jeff to hold her.

Jeff pointed to the kid. "He came in and let his beast loose on us. He'd have killed her little dogs and us too if I hadn't been able to grab the monster."

"As if," the kid snorted.

"Luckily we were in the neighborhood when someone called 911. The operator clearly heard you say you were going to let Wolf rip out someone's throat. Those words constitute a threat, and it is clear, this dog is a menace," the first deputy said.

Jeff glanced at Jessica as she patted her pockets for her phone. She didn't find it. She remembered dialing for help but never said a word as she grabbed her dog and bag and escaped. The phone must be in the car now.

The second officer put a hand on his gun. "You call him off, or I'll drop him right here."

"Wolf." The next words were in another language. The kid smirked, but the dog did little to quiet.

An animal control truck joined the growing vehicles clogging the street.

The officers loaded the mongrel as the kid ranted. "You can't take my dog. Didn't do nothin' to no one."

As Jessica watched, Jeff came up behind her and wrapped her in his arms. She spun in his hold, still hugging herself, and buried her face in his shoulder.

"Jess, you're shaking." He rubbed her back.

"I kept imagining that creature attacking you."

Jeff chuckled. "You don't hope, but you can imagine the worst?"

She dared look up at him. "I had at least two dozen worst case scenarios hit me at once."

Jeff tucked her tight against himself again and kissed the top of her head. "I'm all right." He rubbed her back and her muscles relaxed. "Though we seem to be setting a bad precedent."

She glanced up again.

"Two nights in a row, the cops have needed to intervene."

"Do you think God is trying to send us a message?"

Jeff stared at her. "No." He pulled her close again. "Well ... maybe He wants to show us we need each other. If you hadn't been there last night, who knows what I would have been accused of. It makes me sick to think what could have happened to you if I hadn't been here tonight."

Jessica pulled from him. "But if we hadn't been together, you wouldn't have given a thief your phone to take our picture and I would be at home right now."

The second sheriff came toward them as the first restrained the kid who cussed and tried to get to his dog. "You two all right?"

"Shaken." Jeff said. "But not stirred—I meant in one piece."

The deputy grinned. "Good. Can you tell me what happened?" He took out a note pad and recorded what Jeff said.

"We had enjoyed a nice dinner and her dogs were playing happily as the kid arrived—"

"Those two little rats, challenged Wolf. Set him off," the kid shouted.

"Miss Easton, immediately restrained her pets, but he let his monster loose—"

"The leash slipped out of my hands."

Jeff ignored the continued interruptions. "He released it on purpose, in order to do us harm, as the 911 operator clearly heard."

As the exchange between Jeff and the kid proceeded and the officer took notes, Jessica added little. Her mind drifted back to their earlier conversation. If they hadn't been together, none of it would have happened. Did it mean something she couldn't—or didn't want to—grasp? She had the spiritual insight of a sidewalk. How did you recognize an event as a message from God versus living in a messed up world?

She tried to picture what it would be like if she'd never met Jeff. She would have gone to the office on Monday. Kevin would have succeeded in guilting her into doing some or all of his report, but her work environment would be better for her now.

But the Hansen's house wouldn't be as far along. Jeff would still be hiding in his hoodie, buried in shame. She wouldn't be considering a web design business. The obvious difference is she wouldn't be in …

As the officer finished, she glanced back at Jeff. He'd slipped his arm around her and pulled her close. Their gazes locked.

Wouldn't be in … what?

"I'm not sorry," he said.

"About what?"

"Any of it. It was worth having my phone almost stolen to get a few shots of you and us together. Almost getting eaten by a ferocious dog came after a nice homemade meal. Think what would have happened if Wolf had run into a little kid tonight instead. The animal is off the streets. The entire neighborhood is safer because you changed my world."

Emotions and thoughts hit her from every side like being the last one in a dodge ball game against giants. Her head hurt, her heart beat an erratic tempo, yet she only wanted Jeff's arms wrapped around her.

He leaned forward and his lips pressed against hers. His tender, sweet kiss ended before she realized what happened. He'd kissed her. For the first time in almost thirty years, she'd been kissed.

He enfolded her in his comforting embrace. Nothing made sense, but this felt right. She relaxed against him.

He stroked her back. "It's all going to work out, Jess." He kissed the top of her head and held her as everyone else left.

Chapter 28

Jess pulled in behind him as Jeff closed his truck door. "Hey."

"Hey."

He considered her subdued greeting, and the dim smile. She wore her hair up again and had dressed in an old t-shirt splattered with a few different colors of paint. A cancer walk logo adorned the front.

He kissed her sweet lips as he slipped his arm around her. Again, she seemed surprised and didn't engage in the romantic gesture. "You all right?"

"Didn't sleep well."

"Why?"

"Let's just say, if the cops show up today, we'll have to reconsider our time together."

He pulled her to a stop. "I thought we had an agreement. Carpe diem."

"Seize the day?"

"Yes, *the* day. This day. A single day. Not the past or all future days. *The* day."

She expelled a long breath. "It just seems beyond hard."

"Today, I get to be with a beautiful, smart, talented, woman as we slap some drywall mud on the walls we put up. What's hard about that?"

She rewarded him with a smirk, but didn't argue for once. She, at least, showed some progress.

"Friends." A petite, dark haired woman ducked under the rising garage door. She threw out her arms. "Oh, thank you. We're grateful for your help again." Her words were lightly seasoned with a hint of an accent.

"Rosa." Jess gave her a hug. "How are you all doing?"

Rosa released Jess and moved to Jeff and hugged him tight as well. Since meeting Jess, so much of his life had changed.

"Blessed, because of good friends like you. Come." She waved them through the garage and into the kitchen.

Jeff spotted all the supplies in the corner.

"David came last evening." She pointed to the premixed drywall compound, tape, pans, and various sized knives. "He says that's all you should need. Would you like us to move these?"

Jeff turned to the refrigerator in the middle of the space and a stool with a microwave perched on it. He shook his head. "We might unplug the microwave, but they are far enough away from the walls to give us plenty of room to work."

"You sure?"

"Yes, it's fine."

"Okay, I'll get out of your way, but I have a big lunch planned."

"Rosa, you don't have to—" Jess started to say.

"And you two didn't have to come and work on my house on your Saturday. Work a little and then we'll eat."

"Yes, ma'am." Jeff inclined his head with a smile.

She slapped the air, "Oh, you. Rosa. You call me Rosa. No, ma'ams here."

She disappeared and Jeff turned to Jess.

She shrugged as she stared at all the supplies. "I have no idea."

"Good, then I get to impress you a little today."

"You astonish me all the time."

Jeff paused to look at her. She raised a brow as if to challenge his surprise. "All right then. Here's a mud lesson." He scooped a little of the compound into a pan with the smallest of the knives. With slow movements, he showed her how to draw some out on one side, swipe it over a screw head embedded in the wall. Then he cleaned off her knife on the opposite edge of the pan before he repeated the process again. Next he held the pan and allowed her to try. He put his hand over hers to help her get the right angle and pressure. On the fourth screw she didn't require his help anymore. Somehow, her independence both made him proud and disappointed.

"You work on those while I get a seam prepared, then I'll need your help to get the tape in place."

She continued on without a word and had all the screws on one wall covered before he needed her.

He smeared a little mud from the tip of his finger onto her nose. "All right Speedy Gonzales. Unless you plan on deserting me and leaving early, you can slow down a mite."

She startled at his playfulness. Her gaze narrowed. She put her fingers in the mud and flicked it at him.

Jeff laughed. He lowered his hand to the near full bucket of compound and eyed her.

"Don't you dare," she squealed.

"Are you two working or playing?" Rosa laughed as she opened the fridge and pulled out a pitcher of lemonade.

"Can't we do both?" Jeff said still with his hand hovering over the mud.

Rosa glanced from him to Jess and back again, a knowing smile grew wide. "Si, you have your fun. There is ice cold lemonade and a hose in the backyard when you are finished." She chuckled as she passed through the sheet hanging where the sliding glass door would go.

Jess put up her hands in surrender and backed away from him. "You wouldn't."

"Depends. Are you going to stop being perfect at every task you try?"

She stared for a moment. Her shoulders squared, chin came up, and she crossed her arms. "No."

Jeff straightened from the mud and smiled. "Good. Because you're pretty awesome. Or pretty *and* awesome. Both of those."

"Thanks," she whispered—but again she hadn't argued. Definite progress.

They followed Rosa out to collect a cool drink. "You or a loved one?" Jeff asked.

Jess' brow crinkled, and he pointed to her t-shirt for the cancer walk. She glanced down. "Oh, a former coworker. Breast cancer. She's a ten-year survivor now, I think. I haven't talked to her in a few years. She moved closer to family and we kind of lost touch."

"My mom died of kidney cancer," he said.

"I'm sorry."

Jeff shrugged. "It happened a long time ago. She met both my girls, but never knew about the accident."

"You really need to forgive yourself." She took a full cup from Rosa.

He grabbed one too, and they turned back toward the house. "I wish I could get their forgiveness."

"Your girls?"

"Well maybe. Who I really need forgiveness from, is the people I hurt."

Chapter 29

Jeff and Jessica made quick progress. The mud on the kitchen walls would have to dry before another coat could be added. She checked her watch. "Still a half an hour till lunch and only the ceiling left. Looks like we'll finish early. What should we do?" Something like excitement tickled insider her.

Jeff pulled his phone from his pocket, entered the number, and put it on speaker.

"Hello?"

"Hey, David. It's Jeff and Jess. Sorry to bother you, but we're almost done with the mudding for today. Do you want us to hang the drywall in the garage before we leave?"

"Dang, what time did you all get there?"

"It's just the two of us, and about nine," Jessica said as she glanced at Jeff who smiled ridiculously big at her.

"Either I have the lamest crew in town, or you two are the wonder twins. You're crazy fast. You put five inches of mud on *all* the drywall joints and the tape too, right?"

"We only have the ceiling to finish, but Jess covered all the screws."

"Man, can't believe you did a full first coat already. Yeah, sure, if you feel up to tackling the garage too—have at it. The more you get done, the faster the Hansens will be back to normal. Thanks, you two."

"Sure." They both said at the same time.

Jeff hung up, slid the phone back in his pocket, and walked into the garage. "Jess?"

His tone didn't sound good.

"How do you feel about firefighters showing up?"

"What?" She joined him as a fire engine rumbled to a stop at the end of the drive, the air brakes hissed, and several men stepped out.

"Hi there," a young man said as he pushed his fingers through his hair. "Is Rosa or Stephen—"

A giggled squeal came from behind Jessica as Rosa flew past them and hugged each of the firefighters. She babbled excitedly making it hard to understand her.

The first firefighter stepped a little closer to Jeff and extended his hand. "Casey, nice to meet you."

Jeff took it. "Hi. I'm Jeff and this is Jessica. We're lending a hand with the repairs."

"We were the ones called out about the fire here. Rosa has brought goodies by the station house at least once a week since. We had a call-out around the corner and thought we'd stop by and tell her thanks in person."

Rosa scampered to them and clapped her hands like a kid. "You have to come see." She waved the firefighters into the kitchen and Jeff and Jessica followed. "Look!"

"Wow, work is finally moving along," Casey said. "Nice job."

"Do you know the cause of the fire?" Jessica asked.

"A short in the wiring behind the stove," a dark-haired, older man said.

"The outlet hadn't been overloaded?" Jeff glanced at Jessica with a raised brow.

"No. Only the stove could access the outlet behind it," the man confirmed.

"Rosa, has the insurance company still refused to pay?" Jessica asked.

"Yes. They haven't paid. Say it's our fault."

Casey reached out his hand to Rosa. "Give me your adjustor's number. I'll make sure they have a copy of our report. We'll get this cleared up."

"Really? Thank you. Oh, you all are wonderful. Oh, bless you. God bless each and every one of you." Rosa vanished to retrieve the contact and returned a moment later. "Now we have lunch ready in the backyard. Come, come."

"We have to get back to the station, but thanks, Rosa." Casey held up the insurance information. "I'll make sure they have all the documentation to get your payout to you right away." The men waved goodbye and Rosa swiped at a tear as she urged Jeff and Jessica out to eat.

Jeff's arm slid around Jessica. "Now, see? If we hadn't hooked up, I wouldn't be here today working. If I hadn't come today, you wouldn't be here with me. No one would have asked the firefighters about the fire's cause and the Hansens would still be fighting with the insurance company. Carpe Diem."

Jessica fought the raging heat crawling up her neck and into her cheeks. "We don't use the phrase 'hooking up' anymore," she whispered.

Jeff slowed and stared at her. "Okay?"

"It means something way different than what it did when we were growing up."

"Like …"

She fought to swallow and avoided his gaze. "It's what we would have said to refer to as … to you know … going all the way."

"Oh! Good to know." Jeff chuckled. "A little slip of the tongue like that in front of their daughter could have been awkward." He raised his chin toward Rosa and her teen daughter as they filled plates with beans, rice, enchiladas, salad, and more.

He took the overloaded plate and moved to the retaining wall where she had heard his confession. "Aside from my inappropriate innuendo, did you hear the rest of what I said?"

"Yes, we had a good day."

"*Any* day with you is a good day," Jeff smiled and bumped his shoulder into hers.

She felt the same. Days spent with him were good. Carpe diem, be bold. Her life had changed and for once she liked it—as long as she didn't look too far ahead. Still, she wished she knew how to make it last. What should she say and do? She had to get control of this run-away circus car before all the monkeys broke loose and ran wild. She could envision them swinging from the chandelier and screeching until she wanted to cover her ears.

Where did that come from? Monkeys? Seriously? Jeff had turned her world into a circus and it messed with her head.

Chapter 30

The following day, Jeff slipped in front of Jess after the service as they headed in opposite directions. "I want to talk to David about what we got done yesterday. Meet you in a minute."

"Thank you again for all you've done to help over at the Hansen's place," David said kneeling on the stage.

Jeff scanned through the shots he'd taken on his phone yesterday and showed them to David. "I've had a lot of fun. It's been a good way to get to know Jess better."

David laughed. "A sure way to see anyone's real character is to do a home improvement project together." He took the phone for a closer look. "Did you finish all the dry wall?"

"I think so. We covered every bare stud I could find except the ceiling in the garage. Rosa said it had been open before the fire."

David sat his guitar aside and hopped down next to him. "What is it you do exactly?"

"Accounting work for small businesses, install network and data storage systems, and rehabilitate horses for a care center."

"And Jessica?"

"She works for a grant office distributing funds and builds websites."

David handed back the phone. "Then how in the heck did you two complete near a week's worth of construction work in a couple of days?"

"We've both done a lot of home repairs on our separate places. We met at *U Build It*."

"Well if you ever need a job, you're hired. Wait. Did you say Jessica does websites?"

Jeff brought up his site and handed back his phone.

David spent a few minutes clicking through the pages. "Wow. Jessica did this?"

"From scratch. My original site sucked."

David charged away as he passed back the phone which Jeff barely caught. "Where is she?"

"Jessica!" David yelled across the crowd in the foyer.

She turned to him with a raised brow.

"Help," David said, his hands pressed together like he prayed. "Can you fix my website too?"

Jessica looked from him to Jeff.

"She charges about four hundred for a complete makeover."

"I'll pay for it. Business has gotten slow. We need to get our name out there to pull in some more repair jobs."

"Give me the information, and I'll have a look." Jessica startled and her eyes went wide as David wrapped her in a sudden embrace.

"Tomorrow I'll have Sally call you with the site and login information you'll need. Thank you. Thank you so much." David slapped Jeff on the shoulder as he turned back to the sanctuary. "She's a keeper."

Jeff smiled. His sentiments exactly. He slid his hand into hers as they turned to the door.

"Did I hear you do websites?" Pastor Matt said as he hugged Jessica too.

"One. I've done one."

Again, Jeff handed over his phone.

Pastor arched a brow. "Impressive. I'm sure you've heard Marcus is heading off to college in a couple of months. He has kept all the church's social media and the website up-to-date. It's only a few hours per week, but do you think it would be something you'd be interested in?"

"I'll take a look and talk with Marcus, see if I can handle it," Jess said.

"She'll be great at it," Jeff wrapped his arm around her and squeezed.

They moved out into the glare of a California summer. "You say you want to quit your job, and you now have … what? Five offers to do websites? This church gig would be regular hours each week. Isn't this what you church people would call a sign?"

"I suppose so." Jessica offered him a smile.

"Hey, you mind if we swing by my place before lunch? The horse from SoCal came in around midnight, and I wanted to check on him."

"Sure. I'll follow you."

Jessica followed Jeff's truck out of the main part of town. The frequency of the homes decreased, and the land opened up, dotted in neat rows by tall towers suspending electrical lines. They turned down a narrow lane flanked by fields of high brown grass. She shadowed Jeff and drove around a half-circle in front of a gray-green ranch-style home similar to her parents.

He hopped out, waved, and called, "I'll be a minute."

Jessica slipped out of her SUV and followed him through the gate of a corral on the far side of the house. He disappeared into the stable as she arrived. A brown horse with a dark mane and tail munched on hay and looked up, his ears twisted forward as his gaze considered the stranger in his domain. A black horse watched her from a little farther away.

"I'm just visiting. Mean you no harm," Jessica said as softly as possible. The brown one watched her for a few more minutes before he returned to the hay, but the black one never took his eyes off her.

Movement caught her attention, and Jessica turned expecting Jeff, but a marble gray horse ambled toward her with its head down. It lumbered directly for her and didn't seem to acknowledge Jessica stood in its path. A moment of fear gave way to confusion as she tried to step out of the way, but the horse followed. It didn't stop until it pressed its head against her chest. A long breath leaked from the large animal as it stood and leaned into her.

Jessica rubbed its face, and it pushed causing her to take a step back or fall. The animal wouldn't move away, and if Jessica tried to stop petting her, the horse nudged at her hand until she started again. This crazy horse acted like her girls when they were desperate for some affection.

A metal bucket crashed to the ground and startled both Jessica and the horse. They turned to see Jeff, a pile of spilled oats at his feet, as he stood with his mouth agape. "What did you do?"

"What?" Jessica asked as the horse's ears went back and it snorted.

"She's the cantankerous, spiteful, wretched beast who kicked me."

Jessica gasped and covered the horse's ears. "I'd kick you too if you called me names."

Chapter 31

Jeff struggled to make sense of the site before him. Jess stood in his corral, and the hateful mare he considered selling pressed her face against Jess like they were long-lost friends. "That horse wouldn't get anywhere near me. How on earth did you get her to come to you?"

"I didn't," Jess shrugged. "I tried to get out of her way when she wandered over, but she followed. When I stopped and stood still, she rested against me."

"Unbelievable."

"Maybe she's like Toffee. She doesn't like men."

His horse Ranger strolled toward him and hoped to get the oats He'd had dropped. Jeff pushed his face away. "You don't need any." He cleaned up what he could and inched to the newcomer, the black gelding at the back of the corral. The mare stayed close to Jess, but watched his every move.

The gelding sniffed the air, clearly seemed interested in what Jeff had, but he didn't care to come nearer. As Jeff closed the gap between them, the horse turned and trotted a few feet away to maintain his distance.

Jeff poured the oats into a larger tub and backed up. "Come on, boy. I won't hurt you."

The mare neighed from her place near Jess.

"Oh, shut up you. I didn't ask your opinion," Jeff shouted back.

The mare moved as if to put Jess between her and Jeff.

It made Jess laugh. "She really doesn't like you."

"I've noticed." He came back toward them and the mare stiffened as if she might bolt. "I want to try something, if you're game."

"O-kay." Jess didn't sound convinced.

Jeff put a saddle blanket on the fence. "See if she will let you put it on her."

Jess retrieved it, and she let the horse inspect it before she slowly slid it onto her back. The mare turned and considered it but didn't seem to mind otherwise.

"Now try this." He pointed to the saddle he'd placed on the fence.

Jeff watched, unable to assist because of the hateful mare, as Jess struggle to find the best way to hold it and lift it off. She again let the crazy animal check it. After a few grunts, Jess raised the saddle to the horse's back. The mare continued to stand there, though she always kept an eye on Jeff.

He instructed Jess how to connect and tighten the cinch.

"Oh." Jess' hand brushed lightly over the mare's flank.

Jeff tried to move toward her, but the horse snorted and stepped away. "What is it?"

"There's a patch with no hair. It looks scarred."

"It's right where spurs would hit."

Jess turned to him. "I bet this is what caused her hatred of men."

"Some man caused her a lot of pain."

She rubbed the mare's face. "Poor thing."

Jess finished, and Jeff provided the bridle next and the cranky mare took it without a fuss. "Lead her over to the hay bales at the end of the stable. See if she lets you mount."

"And if she doesn't?"

"Then you'll be on the bales—shorter distance to fall and a soft landing."

"Gee, thanks."

"I have a good feeling about this. You've done more with her in the last twenty minutes than I have in the last month."

The mare craned her neck around to watch Jess as closely as she could. Jess put one foot in the stirrup and paused. She added some weight without leaving the bale. Still, the horse remained unmoved. "You do remember I said it's been years since I've ridden?"

"It's like riding a bike."

"I haven't done that in even longer, and my bike could never toss me aside and trample me."

He hoped his curiosity wouldn't put Jess in danger. Maybe they shouldn't try this. He'd never forgive himself if his stunt injured her. He opened his mouth to tell Jess to stop when she put all her weight in the stirrup and swung her other leg over.

The mare shifted her stance, turned, and sniffed at Jess' feet. She hadn't come dressed for riding in her lacy tank top, white short pants, and backless sandals, but there she sat atop a horse Jeff had been convinced could never be ridden.

"How does she feel?"

"Large."

Jeff chuckled. "No, is she tight, or relaxed?"

"It's hard to tell because *I'm* not very relaxed at the moment."

"Can you get her to move? Don't kick her though."

"Ya think?" Jess shot him a sassy look and he smiled. She used the reins, clicked her tongue, and moved the mare away from the stable and into the middle of the corral.

"You're amazing."

Jess stared at him; brows drawn tight together. "Because the horse hasn't dumped me on my bum?"

He chuckled. "Yeah, you have a way with her."

He approached them, and Jeff reached up to pull Jessica down. The mare side stepped him, snorted and turned in challenge. "Now listen, you cranky beast."

"Oh, don't you mind the grumpy man. He's jealous you like me more." Jess stroked the horse's neck and scratched between her ears, at the same time she smirked at him.

Sassy. The playful woman made him desperate to kiss her. "Well, since she won't let me get close, can you get down on your own?"

Jess stepped down. The stirrups were a bit high, and she almost lost her balance. Jeff lurched forward wrapped her in his arms and pressed his lips to hers. She welcomed him a little more this time but still remained tight. "Looks like you own a horse."

Jess laughed. "Don't think she'll fit in my yard."

"She can stay here ..."

The mare leaned forward and tried to bite Jeff's arm.

Jess made a tone to indicate her disapproval. He'd heard her make the same noise to her dogs. It sounded like a game show buzzer but with a sharpness to it, both her small girls and this new large one responded. "Behave," she said to the mare who snorted at her.

"Yes, behave and you can stay, and Jess will visit all the time."

The horse tossed its head and nudged Jess with her snout. She looked at Jess as if she wanted to leave with her and never come back.

"Now I have to share you with two dogs *and* a horse. This relationship is getting crowded."

Jess avoided his stare and by pushing the meddlesome horse away again.

"Hey, I have an idea. Let's go in the house, pack a lunch, and take the horses for a ride."

"As long as it's not too far. It really has been a very long time since I've ridden. I only sat in the saddle for a few minutes, and I can feel it."

Jeff kissed her again before he released her. Her lips were a little softer each time and welcomed him more. "You coming?"

"No." She turned to the mare and rubbed her face and neck as the horse leaned against her again. "You know many little girl's dream is to have their own pony. I'll stay with mine."

"You don't want to come inside? What if you don't like the way I make your sandwich?"

"You know me, I'm not picky. Whatever you make will be fine." Jess ignored him as she turned her full attention to the horse.

Chapter 32

Jeff slid in his backdoor and headed to the fridge. Earlier in the week, Jess hadn't invited him to her home, instead they met at the dog park. Next she'd refused to let him pick her up. Now, she wouldn't come into his house either. Did this have something to do with the 'I don't do hope' rule or did she have another reason to avoid him? How can I date a woman who dodges me?

Jeff washed his hands and started a sandwich assembly line as his mind continued to work the puzzle of Jess' behavior. She melts into my arms when I hold her, but her kisses are not what anyone would consider passionate. She goes out with me, but there is always an invisible barrier between us. She's alluded to the fact she hasn't dated much. Could I be seeing her inexperience? An awkward teen in her first relationship, navigating her first dates? Maybe Jess just isn't into me. Or I could be moving too fast for her.

By the time the lunches were prepared, Jeff had almost talked himself out of the horseback ride. Jess and he weren't going to work as a couple. But when he rounded the stable and she looked up. Her smile welcomed him, and his apprehension evaporated in its warmth. "Does she have a name yet?"

Jess scratched the mare's forehead. "Storm."

Jeff paused as he carried his saddle toward Ranger.

"She's marbled gray like a stormy sky, and storms can be violent and dangerous." Jess smirked at him, "or gentle and refreshing," she said as she hugged Storm's face.

Jeff shook his head and set his saddle atop Ranger. "You are brilliant. It hurts to think about how much smarter you are than me."

Jess shrugged, "Like I said, I have a weird brain."

As Jeff finished saddling his horse and storing their lunch, she led Storm back to the hay bales and mounted again. He noted when he drew alongside her, she now wore tennis shoes.

"Smart," he said with a nod.

"Glad I forgot to take them out of the car Friday. I usually take one of my breaks and walk around the building or up and down the stairs. But Friday, Kevin kept me busy during my breaks, and at lunch I went to a coffee shop to work on Shannon's site." She wiggled her foot drawing his attention to her shoe again.

They rode to the rear of his property, and Jeff leaned down to undo the gate. Storm kept an eye on him, which meant Jess couldn't get the animal to ride abreast of him but back a few feet. The horse seemed calm and unbothered by Jess riding her though. Once he secured the gate behind them, they turned toward the distant tree line, and rode in silence for several moments.

"It may have been a while, but you have good form. Storm continues to remain calm with you."

"I think we have both been able to relax a little. Glad the weather isn't another sizzling day too."

Jessica stepped out of her car with a wince. Though they hadn't ridden for long yesterday, she still hobbled with a bit of a bow in her legs. She moved with care as she lifted each foot to the next step and it took longer as her legs trembled. She used the stairs to her floor, instead of the elevator, in hopes her muscles would loosen along the way.

"We have to get to the meeting." The door to her work area hadn't even closed behind her before Kevin barked orders. He stood outside his office, arms crossed, and gaze narrowed.

"We have thirty minutes to get one floor up. I'll put my purse and bag down, clock in, and scan my emails. I'll be there on time."

A sharp exhale accompanied his snarled lips. "Well, I need to inform you, the copier is down."

"All right." Jessica continued on to her cubicle and dropped her purse in the bottom drawer. She'd brought her laptop to work on a few websites during lunch but sat it on her desk.

After she logged into her company computer, she clocked in, and popped open her email. With a quick scan through them she deleted the junk. Kevin moved away from his monitor to talk to Yolanda. Jessica took advantage of his momentary distraction and sent the template she needed to her personal email. By the time Kevin returned to his desk, she had the form open on her laptop as she sporadically clicked on random work emails on her company computer.

She dropped in the few figures she had written on a notepad last week and saved the document.

"We are going to be late," Kevin called.

Good grief, did he tap his foot as he waited? She slid her laptop into the meeting binder and stood. "I'm ready." She walked beside him as he sneered, and they headed for the elevator.

"Wow, you two are eager this morning," Vicki said as she entered the conference room ten minutes later. She took the seat across from Jessica and smiled. "How was your weekend?"

"Good, a—" What did she call Jeff? An acquaintance? Friend? Boyfriend—definitely not! "A new friend and I mudded some drywall at the house of a church member who suffered a fire a little while back."

One of Vicki's brows rose. "Working on drywall? This is what you call fun weekend activities?"

Jessica laughed. "I actually had a lot of fun. I learned a lot, and I like helping Rosa and her family get back into their house. Yesterday, we ended up at his place and went riding. He even gave me a horse."

"He?" The question lingered in the air between them.

Heat flashed across Jessica's face. She swallowed hard as the two directors entered and took their seats.

"Sorry we're late. We were trying to connect to a new donor." Paul the taller of the two men had the skinniest limbs. Jessica figured he had to buy tailor-made items. He would swim in clothes off the rack. He brushed a hand over his thin blond hair and settled into his seat.

Frank had dark hair and always wore a suit and tie. She couldn't imagine him at the gym in shorts and a t-shirt, but his build told her he must work out. While Frank pictured a polished businessman, he rarely spoke. He let Vicki and Paul direct their meetings.

Vicki started with her portion, and reported on their various grants they were currently accepting requests for. Paul informed them of the funding coming in, and then they turned to Jessica.

Kevin rocked back in his chair at the end of the oval table. Another sneered filled his face as he stared at her.

"We seem to have a problem with our copier downstairs." Jessica said as though printer breakdowns happened all the time—which it didn't.

"Oh, that's odd," Vicki said.

"We'll call the service provider as soon as we conclude here," Paul said.

"If you don't mind, I have the report ready and can display it on the screen." She pointed behind Kevin to the blank space on the wall they used for a screen. "I will also email you a copy later to have until the machine is repaired."

"Please, go right ahead," Frank nodded with a small smile.

Jessica popped open her laptop as Kevin's jaw gaped. She connected the cable, and soon the pie charts of where their money had been distributed in the last month filled the screen. She reported on the different accounts and explained each and where they stood on available funds.

"I prefer this over the hard copies none of us keeps, anyway. We all get the files electronically at some point—why not present this way from now on?" Frank said more than Jessica had ever heard in all the time she'd worked for him.

She smiled, took her seat, and let the screen go grey as she closed her computer.

Vicki and Paul heartily agreed, and Kevin turned the same shade as a fire truck. Not only had she done the report when he'd tried to block her every effort, but she'd also revolutionized their meetings.

Vicki turned to Kevin now who sat with his arms still crossed. "And how is the application collection going for the new funds and the remainder of these accounts?"

Kevin glared at Jess. "I never received the data I needed to create my report."

All eyes turned to Jessica.

This is how you want to play it? Very well. She opened her computer again, and the screen on the wall mirrored the image in front of her. Without a word she logged on to her company email and opened her sent items. "As you can see, I sent all the needed information to Mr. Perry on Tuesday. Here is the reminder I sent on Thursday and a final update on Friday. From this indication here on each, you can see Mr. Perry not only received each email, he opened all of them."

Every head turned back to face Kevin. They stared wordlessly at him as he glared at Jessica.

"Jessica, thank you for all your hard work. I think we have some concerns to discuss which you do not need to be bothered with at this time. I'll talk to you later." Vicki smiled at her as Jessica collected her laptop and binder and slipped from the tension-filled room.

Chapter 33

Jessica plopped in her desk chair, her binder and laptop rested in her lap. She stared at her work computer. The screen had gone to sleep and her reflection gazed back at her. *Now what?*

Kevin and his antics would result in one of two outcomes: they were upstairs firing him, or they were putting him on a written improvement plan. *Will either of those work out for me?*

If Kevin's fired, I have to take up all his work until a new boss is hired and no doubt they'll try to get me to step into the job. I don't want it. I don't want the one I have. But if they keep him, which seems more like their style, then I'll have to work with a man who will forever hate me. She sighed and her posture deflated into a slouch.

"Miss Jessica?"

She looked up to see Ian over her cubicle wall. "Hey, you need me?"

"You okay?" Ian was having a good day. In those moments when his disabilities didn't inhibit his personal connections, Ian could be one of the most observant people to others' emotions.

"It's been a long week already."

He tipped his head and considered her. "It is Monday morning."

"True, it is. But it feels like late Friday night with a grant submission window closing in an hour."

"I hate those days."

"Me too."

"But you are all right?"

"I think so. Thanks for checking on me."

Ian glanced toward Kevin's office. "Mr. Kevin is not back."

"They needed to talk with him for a moment."

"He is in trouble. He should not yell at you. Yelling is against the rules. No one can yell in the workplace. It makes for a hostile work environment. It lowers morale and it increases stress. Increased stress leads to heart disease, hypertension—"

Jessica put up her hand to try to stop his recitation of the entire training seminar they'd all had to sit through. "You're correct. The workplace should be friendly."

"Miss Jessica is my friend."

"Thank you, Ian. Your kindness means a lot. You're my friend too."

Ian turned away, wandered back to his workspace, and left Jessica to stare at her reflection again. Before she realized what she intended to do, the phone sat pressed to her ear. "Hi, Vicki? You have a minute?"

Jessica stepped into Vicki's office. The conference room across the hall still had the door closed.

"The men are working out a mentoring schedule with Kevin. He says he still wants to work here," Vicki said with a smile.

"Oh, it's none of my business."

"As it has impacted you, I'd say it is." She leaned back in her chair, but her dark eyes didn't sparkle as they held her in a somber gaze.

"I'm giving my notice, Vicki."

Her deep maroon lips lowered in a frowned. "I feared it would come to this. We will work with him. This won't happen again."

"I know. You have all been great. I'm fifty-years-old now, and it's time for a change. I've been thinking about it for a while. It isn't personal."

Vicki leaned forward, the lime green of her blouse clashed with the array of colored file folders on her desk. She smiled in the way that said girl-talk time had begun, and not business. "What do you have in mind?" Her voice vibrated with excitement.

"I think I'm going to design websites."

Vicki sat up a little straighter, brows high. "Really?"

Jessica chuckled. "Don't sound so surprised. I worked on the one here for a few years. I redid a friend's and since then I've gotten several requests to revamp others."

"You worked on the grant site?"

Jessica nodded.

"Why'd you stop?"

"When they hired Manuel, Frank gave the work to him. Said Manuel had the proper training and I could go back to focusing on my intended job." After all these years the comment still stung.

Vicki placed her finger on her keyboard. "What site have you done?"

Jessica gave her the URL for Jeff's landing page and Vicki typed. "Since I have a large amount of sick time banked, perhaps I could vacation out after my two weeks."

Vicki didn't seem to hear her. "You did this? Seriously? Just you?"

"Yeah, something wrong?"

Vicki shook her head. Her gaze narrowed and lips scrunched to one side. She got the same look any time she had the beginnings of an idea yet struggled to make all the pieces fit together. "It's almost eleven. Do me a favor and take an early lunch. Go off sight and enjoy a cool ice tea. Come back here at one."

Jessica opened her mouth to question, but she knew better. When Vicki got like this, you couldn't rush her. She'd get all her ducks in a row before she revealed that in fact, she had race cars lined up for a cross-country excursion. Jessica nodded, returned to her desk to grab her laptop and purse, and headed for the corner coffee shop.

Chapter 34

Jeff used the back of his arm to rid his brow of sweat. He pulled open his backdoor and stepped into the cool interior as his phone chimed. In the hot days of summer, he usually worked with the horses in the morning, came in for lunch, then spent the rest of the afternoon on his computer in front of a fan with the AC on high. Today the time had gotten away from him as he tried to coax the newest horse to allow him to get close.

He pulled water from the fridge with one hand and his phone from his back pocket with the other.

Jessica: "I quit my job."

Jeff almost dropped the water pitcher. "Where are you?" he texted back.

"Just pulled in my driveway."

"I'm on my way."

His phone chimed repeatedly, but he didn't look at it as he drove to her place. He knew what each said. "Don't come." "Let's meet *somewhere*." No. This time he intended to go to her place.

He'd found her address in a church directory he'd picked up a few weeks back. He turned into her neighborhood of mostly single-story homes from the seventies. All of them were painted in light colors. Jess' house sat at the top of a T-intersection near a cross street. Unlike her immediate neighbors, her garage jutted forward from the rest of the structure. She'd painted it a dark tan with pine green trim.

She stood outside with her girls on their leashes. *I still don't get to go in your house.* It felt off, but he pulled into the drive and stepped out.

"You didn't have to come all the way over here." She smiled though it didn't reach her eyes. "Not sure how you knew where I lived either."

He held up the church directory before he closed his door.

Her smile brightened with a bit of a smirk. "Oh."

"I wanted to hear all about it. Make sure you were all right." As he approached, both dogs barked. After a sniff, Licorice quieted and sprang up to Jeff's hip to get him to pick her up. Toffee backed up as far behind Jess as her lead would allow and howled. "Hush you," Jeff said and gave Jess a kiss. The dog yawled all the more.

Jess leaned against the garage, and now pushed off as they started down the driveway. "It's crazy. I'm not sure I believe it."

Licorice bounded in every direction and stopped frequently causing Jeff to trip. "Here, why don't I take her?"

"She's little, but she'll jerk your arm out of its socket. She can stop and start on a dime."

"I've been warned," he said his hand still extended for the leash as he stepped over it again. "Now, what happened. Did good ol' Kevin let you finish your report?"

"No." She proceeded to tell him about how Kevin had waited for her to arrive, urged her to the meeting early, and declared the copier was down. Jeff's anger dissipated and his chest puffed out as she told him about how she got the report done regardless and showed Kevin up in front of the bosses. Jeff loved her intelligence and spunk.

"Even after your triumph, you quit on the spot?"

She laughed as they turned the corner. "After I considered my options of training a new boss or working for one who hated me, I went to Vicki and gave my notice. She asked what I planned to do. When I mentioned websites and the work I've done on a few sites, Vicki checked out your site. She didn't say much before she sent me to lunch early. She told me to come back at one."

They crossed the street and continued down the road he used to enter her neighborhood. "And …?"

Jess stopped and stared at him a moment. "She told me she'd talked with Paul and Frank, and I don't have to come into the office again. As long as I take over the grant website immediately, they'll pay my full wage and insurance for six months until my accrued sick-leave is paid out."

"Wow! That's amazing."

"Oh, you haven't even heard all of it." Thankfully she started walking again. If they hadn't Licorice would have forced him to move or be hauled along after her. "At the end of six months, I'll switch to an hourly wage for the website work and to assure all submissions meet the guidelines. They'll also continue to pay all my insurance until a year from today."

"Sounds like they value you."

"Or they were feeling guilty for what happened with Kevin."

He laced his fingers with hers and kissed the back of her hand. "No, they realize what they just lost. You're amazing."

She stepped off the sidewalk onto the grass of a small park, plopped down on a picnic bench, and pressed her back against the table. "I can't believe I'll continue to earn my full income until after the first of next year. My biggest fear of how I would pay for health insurance is not even a concern—for a year. What company offers a severance package with these kinds of perks?"

Jeff eased down next to her. "One who now sees having you, even part-time, is better than not at all." He touched her chin with a finger and turned her face until he could claim her lips. She tasted sweet and readily kissed him back.

"How should we celebrate?"

Her cheeks flushed. "What did you have in mind?"

"Whatever you want? Dinner, movie, horseback ride—name it."

She searched his face for a long moment. He wished he knew what she was thinking. "Can we sit here for a while?" She slid closer and nuzzled into his one-armed hug. Her head rested on his shoulder, and she let out a long sigh as her weight pressed against him.

"This is all you want?"

"This is all I've ever wanted."

Chapter 35

Jeff had convinced her they should go out to dinner to celebrate, but she still didn't allow him in the house. She unhooked the girls and let them in but only stepped in far enough herself to grab her purse. She locked up, and he opened his pickup door for her.

They'd had a great meal at her favorite seafood restaurant along the river followed by a long stroll. Jess cuddled close and her words, "This is all I ever wanted," echoed through his head again. This—walking or holding hands or cuddling next to each other—such a small request. Didn't she want more? And if not, how come?

When he pulled back in her driveway, she leaned over and kissed him for the first time. "Thank you."

Her action surprised him. "For?"

"For encouraging me, believing in me, celebrating with me. Only my parents have ever offered me this kind of support."

He caressed the side of her face. Her eyes closed and she leaned into his touch. A look of contented peace filled her. She behaved like a person who had lived in a quarantine bubble all her life, and now she could have contact with others.

Jeff pressed his lips to hers, and she responded to him again with an answered kiss. "May I come in?"

She pulled from him, eyes wide, and cheeks bright in a full blush. She shook her head several times before she spoke. "The house is a mess." She fumbled for the door handle. "In truth, I'm a terrible housekeeper." Her words came almost as fast as her gasped breaths. Panic attack. The mere request to come inside sent her scrambling to get away in a hasty, anxiety-laden frenzy.

"I had a great time." She forced a smile to her lips as she gulped air.

Jeff remained buckled behind the steering wheel and hoped she'd relax. "Since you work from home now, you'll have to come over a couple of times each week and give Storm some exercise."

Jess closed the door but held onto the open window. Her shoulders lowered, and she breathed easier. A genuine smile returned. "I think I'd enjoy those rides. The more I do it the less I'll hobble afterwards." She chuckled. "I could barely get out of bed this morning."

"We only rode for about thirty minutes."

"I know. I tried to tell you, I'm in terrible shape."

Jeff smiled. "Your shape is perfect."

She shied away from him, pink flooding her cheeks again. "And I say you've spent way too long with horses."

He hated when she put herself down and didn't take his compliment. But, in reality, she had been as alone and isolated as he had. She, too, seemed to crave the touch of another person. Jess needed his love as much as he needed hers.

"Do we have a date for the morning? Head out before it gets too hot?"

She turned and a smirk danced on her lips. "As long as it isn't *too* early. I never intend to set my alarm again."

He laughed. "One of the best parts of working for yourself is to set your own schedule. How does ten sound?"

"Perfect. See you in the morning." She stepped away with a wave and watched him back out of the drive. *Make sure I leave before you return inside. That's weird.*

The week went by quickly. Jess had come over on Tuesday and Thursday to ride in the morning. She never came inside afterwards, saying she had to return home and get some work done. "I can't get into a schedule with all this free time. I keep telling myself, 'I can do that later.' And before I know it, it's after eleven in the evening and I've gotten nothing done."

"You've been self-employed for a few days. It will take you a few weeks to get in a good rhythm."

They'd gone to the Hansen's home a couple more times to add additional layers of mud to the seams. Next they'd sand them, and then the walls would be ready to paint.

"Rosa, I hoped we can have all the painting done in another week. Sorry this is taking such a long time," Jess said before they left yesterday.

Now, Jess squirmed beside him as Pastor Matt talked from the book of Ephesians. She usually remained attentive as she dutifully took notes on the bulletin insert, but today she fidgeted. She'd bumped into him a couple of times. Then she rolled her shoulders as if she tried to work the tension out of them. He took her hand and it trembled in his. Jeff looked at her with a raised brow as the closing song began. She forced a half smile.

After greeting Pastor Matt they stepped out into the hot, late July sun. "You all right?"

She took a deep breath. "Will you come with me? I have someplace I want to take you."

"Of course." Worry tickled his insides and made his stomach queasy. But her shoulders came down a little as she led the way to her SUV.

They drove in near silence to a neighborhood forty-five minutes north of church. Jess parked on one side of the street and looked at a dark brown house with tan trim directly across from them.

"Okay, where are we?" Could this be her parents' place? Hadn't she said they lived in the foothills?

She turned to him and bit her lower lip—never a good sign. She took a prolonged deep breath and let it out slowly. "That is the home of the Morgan's. Wanda and Malcolm."

Jeff stared at her, his heart seized, and he couldn't capture any air. She'd found them.

She took his hand and squeezed it. "How many times have you told me, if you could ask for their forgiveness you could move on. Now you have the chance."

Jeff couldn't budge.

Jess bowed her head, and squeezed his hand tighter. "Lord, we know You honor those who are humble before You. Those who seek to make right the wrongs they have done. You have laid it on Jeff's heart to seek the forgiveness of this family who were injured by his actions. Now You have provided the opportunity for him to fulfill this desire. Fill him with Your peace and Your mercy. Draw near to him as he does this difficult task. Go before him and make a way for him to find lasting peace with what cannot be changed. We thank You, Lord, for all You do for us every day. Amen."

Jeff had never heard such a personal prayer. The specific prayer had been said over him. His next breath came easier and another followed. "Will," he swallowed the squeak in his voice and tried again. "Will you come with me?"

"I'll be here praying."

He would have preferred she stayed by his side and hold his hand. But she was right. He needed to do this alone.

He got out of her car on quaking legs, and she gave him a crushing hug before he moved to cross the street. "You've got this. I'll be here waiting when you're done."

He managed to make it to their door without collapsing, but it took almost as long to find the strength to ring the bell.

The door opened within moments, and he stood staring at the woman who had plagued his nightmares for years.

Chapter 36

Her dark cocoa skin glowed, and her deep purple suit shone. She beamed at Jeff. Though she had shorter hair, he had no doubt he looked at the woman he'd hit all those years ago. "May I help you?"

He couldn't find his voice. His heart pounded in his ears, and his chest tightened until he couldn't catch his breath. He wanted to talk to this woman for so long—to beg for forgiveness. Now, Jess had found her, and he couldn't make his mouth work.

"You all right, darlin'?" Her smile never faded.

Jeff wanted her to look at him this way forever. But for him to seek her absolution … She'd hate him. Scream and yell. She had every right.

"Darlin' you don't look well. What can I do for you?" Her kindness soothed him.

"My—" He choked and coughed and tried again. He couldn't control his shaking. "My name is—" He swallowed hard. "My name is Jeff. Jeff Tate." He gulped air and couldn't continue for a moment.

Her gaze went wide, flicked to his scarred arm, and back to his face.

He steeled himself, for clearly, she recognized him. Her arms flew out and encircled him as she crushed him to her buxom form. She patted his back with one hand and held his head to her cheek with the other. "Oh, Mr. Tate. Thank you. Oh, I have waited years to tell you this. Thank you so much."

She released him and bounced on the balls of her feet, but Jeff—left reeling from the hug—nearly fell. She gripped his forearm and turned to the interior of her home. "Malcolm? Malcolm, come quick, son."

As she drew him into the home, a tall, lean, young man entered the room and glanced up from his phone. "Yes, ma'am?"

"Malcolm, come here. *This* is Mr. Tate." Her announcement held such pride.

The young man tossed the phone on the couch and stepped forward with an outstretched hand. "Thank you, sir."

Somehow Jeff managed to take the hand offered.

Malcolm held it in a fearsome grip. "Thank you," his voice an awed whisper.

Jeff shook his head and tried to pull his hand free. He looked from mother to son. "No. No, you don't understand. I—I caused—"

Mrs. Mason took both his hands in hers and gripped them tight. "Oh, we know, darlin'. But you saved us. Oh," she brushed away a tear from his cheek as she still held his other hand. "Oh, I wanted to come see you in the hospital, but they only allowed family. Then they whisked you off to jail in a flash. But we prayed for you."

"Every night," Malcolm said.

"Every single day you were in jail, we prayed for you. We pray for you still."

"But—I, I hurt you, and your son," Jeff stammered.

Malcolm smiled and reached his right hand out again to show Jeff two pink blotches on his otherwise dark skin. "They remind me every day of how blessed I am."

Two girls wandered into the living room and joined them. Mrs. Mason clasped his hand again, and she invited them over. "This is Grace, I was pregnant with her at the time, but didn't know it yet. You saved three lives, Mr. Tate. You need to know, too, Grace wants to be a missionary. Because of you, many more lives will be changed." She coaxed the next girl forward after Grace shook his hand too and offered her thanks. "And this is our youngest, Hope. She is already part of the worship ministry at church leading us in praising our Lord."

"And I'm going to be an EMT, because I want to save lives like you did, sir," Malcolm said.

Jeff shook his head. He couldn't control his tears. "I don't understand how you can forgive me after what I did."

"You made a mistake. Drunk driving is always wrong. But you saved us from our burning car. God used you to mend my marriage and bring us back to God in a powerful way. You may have seen it as a terrible thing, but God turned it into a blessing for us, Mr. Tate."

"Mom! The tickets." Mother and son shared a glance.

"Oh, my boy you're right. Mm-hm," her arm flicked out at her son. "Oh, God knew. He always does." Mrs. Mason raised her hands as if she waved to her ceiling. "Oh, He does work His wonders. Amen."

"Amen," the three children echoed.

Jeff looked at Malcolm, confusion added to his many cascading emotions.

The young man smiled. "I'm graduating early—right before Christmas—and we had to purchase tickets for our families to attend. There won't be a lot of space but we got seven tickets because my gran and gram said they wanted to come. Yesterday, gran fell and broke his hip. They won't be able to fly out here and we're left with two extra tickets."

"But they aren't extra. They were always meant for you," Mrs. Mason said and squeezed his arm again.

"I don't know what to say. I only hoped you could find a way to forgive me and you've ..." his words broke off.

"Oh, we done forgave you years ago, Mr. Tate." Mrs. Mason hugged him again. She held him at arm's length and stared hard at him. "Now, if you didn't know we'd forgive you, why'd you come?"

"I didn't." Jeff accepted the tissue Hope offered. "My girlfriend found you and brought me."

Mrs. Mason put one hand on her hip. "And where is your girl?"

He thumbed his finger toward the door behind him. "Waiting ..."

"I'll go fetch her. What's her name?" Mrs. Mason reached for the front door.

"Jessica."

"I'll get Jessica. Grace set two more places."

A huge man joined them from the kitchen as Mrs. Mason opened the door. He stood at least two feet taller than Jeff and bulging muscles filled his clothes. The floor vibrated as he walked.

"Darrell, we have two more for lunch. Mr. Tate and his girlfriend will be joining us."

The door closed behind as Darrell's gazed shifted to him. "Mr. Tate?"

"Jeff," his voice cracked again.

The distance between them disappeared as Darrel moved forward and engulfed Jeff's hand in his meaty one. He jerked Jeff closer and pounded on his back. "Thank you. Thank you for my family." The big man swiped at his own tear when he released Jeff.

A whirlwind encircled Jeff. Like being caught in a tornado, he sailed end over end with debris hurtling by him. He'd been given the one thing he thought he'd never have. Forgiveness. Not some begrudged, *fine, whatever* kind of absolution, but complete and total forgiveness with a huge heap of gratitude. They had prayed for him. Prayed. *For.* Him. Every day he sat in jail and afterwards. Once Jeff had healed enough to be in general population, he'd been terrified of all the hard-core criminals around him. But they'd left him alone. No one had bothered him. Because of this amazing family's prayers? Why would God do this for him?

Jeff couldn't do more than stand and stare at these people while he fought to contain his grateful tears.

Chapter 37

What an idiot. When would she ever learn? Jessica had sprung terrifying news on Jeff again. This could cause far worse damage than putting up a website without his approval. She'd taken him to the family he'd crashed into all those years ago. He feared how they'd react, and she wouldn't even go with him to the door. Coward. She glanced at her watch. Five minutes since he'd disappeared inside. How long should she wait?

Did she subconsciously hope to sabotage their relationship? If she did enough to damage their bond now, Jeff would dump her like she knew he was going to do. Could she be that self-destructive? The fear of him leaving played havoc in her mind, but the sooner the break up happened the better. She'd been unfair to Jeff. He should end his relationship with her and move on to someone who thought more of him than she clearly did.

What could be going on in there? Were they berating him? Beating him to a pulp?

Oh, why couldn't she leave well enough alone? Could this be more than trying to sabotage their growing relationship? What a demented and cruel person she was. She'd made him confess all his sins on their third meeting, and now she'd thrown him to the wolves under the guise of helping him.

She checked her watch again as she leaned against her fender. Her right knee bounced with her growing panic. Seven minutes. How long should she leave him in there? Maybe she ought to go to the door in hopes of rescuing him. What about calling the cops?

Oh, you're an awful person, Jessica Easton. Jeff should hate you. I hate me.

"Girrrlll!" A voice called out snapping Jessica's head up. An African-American woman with curves upon curves, in a purple skirt suit and blue fuzzy slippers, strode toward her with her arms thrown open wide. "You Jessica?"

Jessica nodded as a crushing hug engulfed her. "Thank you for bringing him to us. The Lord bless you, girl."

Jessica blinked as the woman released her. She couldn't think of a thing to say.

The woman swatted her arm, "Girl, you look as scared as he does. Come on, we have lunch on the table, and you two are joining us."

"We are?"

She gave Jessica a tug. "Oh, relax with yourself. Come, lunch is getting' cold, darlin'."

Jessica grabbed her purse and locked the car as the woman looped their arms "Oh, the Lord is good."

"Every day," Jessica stammered, as the woman led her through the door and to the kitchen.

Jeff stood when she came to the table, as did a young man and his older mirror image. Jeff's eyes were red and puffy. He pulled out a chair next to his and, once they sat, he snatched up her hand and clenched it tight.

Wanda Mason made the introductions, and after her husband said grace over the meal, Mrs. Mason explained what had happened while Jessica waited outside in the throes of a meltdown. She listened as they filled their plates.

"Oh, I'd gotten so mad at this lug-head," she said as she pointed at her husband. "Spittin' nails and seein' red. Scooped up my baby and stormed out of the house. I aimed to forsake my vows and sure enough turn my very back on the Lord. Then this angel here,"—she nodded toward Jeff who sat in rapt attention— "he plowed right into us. Bless his heart. The cars went careening around, and the next thing I know I was lyin' on the ground looking up at his sweet face. I could smell smoke and realized my baby was still in the car. At my scream, Mr. Tate ran toward the flames. I never did pray harder in my entire life. Promised the Lord I return to my husband and work on our relationship."

Darrell put down his silverware and took his wife's hand. His ragged words came as he stared at her. "I met her at the hospital. Black eyes and cuts from the glass, but she had never been more beautiful. I realized how much I could have lost. She stayed in the hospital a couple of days to make sure Grace would be okay. We went to see the pastor on the way home. We needed to get right with the Lord if we were going to make this work."

"What an amazing testimony," Jessica said.

"And all because of your Jeff." Darrell smiled at him. "You two are always welcome at our table. You're family."

"Thank you," Jeff's voice cracked.

Jessica could understand. Never in her wildest dreams would she have considered they would be so—loving. The Masons were God's hands and feet. She enjoyed excellent food and hearty laughter well into the afternoon with them.

When the Masons finally allowed them to leave, after they exchanged phone numbers and emails, Jeff stopped her at the car door. "I don't know how to thank you."

He pulled her into a hug, and she held tight. "God did a miracle for you. I'm honored to have witnessed it."

"It only happened because of you."

"I can't take the credit for what they did. The Morgan family is filled with the Lord." She moved to the driver's seat, settled in, and turned the car back to the church where Jeff's truck waited.

He didn't say much, but he held her hand the whole way. She pulled up next to his pickup and turned to him with a smile.

He started to open the door and stopped, but didn't look at her. "I think I want to read the Bible."

"Okay."

He stepped out and turned back to her before he closed the door. "Thank you. I wish I had better words, but I am more than grateful for today."

"I'm really glad it worked out. It could have totally gone the other way."

Jeff nodded and swayed to his vehicle.

She lowered the passenger window. "Text me when you get home." He didn't look steady.

He nodded and turned the key to bring the truck to life. "I love you," he said through his open window.

It sent a jolt through her heart almost as strong as the first time he'd said it. Her mind whirled at the events of the day as she wondered at his comment. She'd tricked him into going to the Masons' home and abandoned him when he needed her the most. They were the ones who had blessed him with their love and forgiveness. Jessica only watched. But he'd made his proclamation with such conviction it left no doubt in her mind he believed it, meant it, felt it.

Her neglected heart shuddered under the power of his love.

Chapter 38

Jeff hadn't slept well. His mind kept racing over his afternoon with the Masons. The entire event had to have been a dream. No, his brain could never come up with such an amazing ending to the terrible accident he'd caused. Like the earth had completely altered its rotation his life would never be the same again.

He stood at his back window and stared through the glass without seeing his corral or stables. He lifted the cup of coffee to his lips but didn't taste it.

His phone rang capturing his attention. "Hello?"

"Hi, is this Jeff?"

"Yes."

"Hey Jeff, this is Luke Winters from Rivers of Grace. Jessica said you wanted to get started in a Bible study. We have several starting up in a couple of weeks. Do you have a few minutes to meet so we can get you plugged into the right one?"

Jerked into the moment, Jeff sputtered as a flash of anger ripped through him. *She won't even read the Bible with me. Fine. I'm done. If Jessica doesn't want me encroaching in her life*—his thought died. She made no sense.

"Jeff? You still there?"

"Yeah." He didn't want to go to some Bible study with strangers, but he needed to know more about this God whose people forgave him completely. With a sigh, he agreed to meet Luke at a local diner.

All the way there, Jeff argued with himself. *Why am I doing this? Jessica* … well he didn't know about her anymore.

A man smiled and waved as Jeff entered the old-style diner with its checkerboard décor. He stood. "Jeff?"

Jeff nodded, moved toward the table, and accepted the proffered hand.

Luke stood a little taller than him. Gray hair cut in a military style spoke of his age, while tattoos on his muscular forearms spoke of a different life than Jeff had lived. Luke waved him into the opposite side of the booth. "Pie is great here," he said as he settled across from him.

Not quite nine in the morning—a little early for pie. The waitress came by and filled his coffee cup. Jeff held it between his hands and tried to ward off his misgivings with its warmth.

"What makes you want to join a Bible study?" Luke leaned back and considered him with an eager look in his brown eyes.

"Well, I'd hoped to learn a little more with Jessica, but …"

Luke leaned in. "But?"

Jeff glanced up with a sigh. "I don't get her. We've been seeing each other for almost three months. She won't come in my house, or allow me in hers. I'm crazy about her, but she won't even read the Bible with me." His stare slid to the black liquid. He could almost see his own reflection. "Maybe this just isn't going to work out."

"Wow," Luke sat back, his eyes hooded as he stroked his chin.

"Weird, right?"

The ding of the bell telling the waitress the kitchen had a plate ready punctuated his accusation.

"I've heard of couples who don't kiss until the pastor says, 'You may now kiss the bride,' but your Jessica has really taken it to the next level, hasn't she?" Admiration filled his voice.

"What?"

Glass shattered along with Jeff's frustration.

"To my way of thinking, being alone behind closed doors, though not what you may have intended, could lead to your relationship going farther than either of you wants. She has probably been protecting you both from temptation. Even the two of you doing a Bible study alone can become very intimate. Our church encourages one-on-one studies be done with people of the same gender, for this reason." Luke took a sip of his coffee. "You have a wise woman there."

She'd been trying to protect them? He couldn't deny his attraction to Jess, but he hadn't thought … well, maybe he had. But she, as always, considered of what would be best for both of them. Oh, he loved Jessica Easton.

The smell of bacon overwhelmed him as a waitress passed carrying three laden plates.

"Tell me a little of your testimony."

"My what?" Jeff continued to try to wrap his mind around Luke's revelation behind Jess' behavior.

"Testimony. When did you accept Christ?"

"Accept Him for what?"

Luke's smile grew. "Are you saved, Jeff?"

"Saved?" He'd heard Pastor Matt say the same word before. About being a believer and being born a second time. It muddled his thoughts a little.

Luke reached beside him as he pushed his coffee to the end of the table with his other hand. Soon a Bible sat between them, and he spent the next hour and a half explaining what God had done for Jeff, and how Jesus had died to pay for Jeff's sin.

Jeff's heart pounded at a rate it hadn't since the last time he'd ridden a roller coaster. It all clicked, and all those weeks hearing pastor's messages finally made sense.

Yesterday, the Masons had lifted a weight of guilt that had crushed him for eighteen years. But as he walked beside Luke toward their cars now, Jeff swam in a peace he had never known. He'd given his life to Christ. Whatever happened from now on would turn out fine. He had found the answers to existence and nothing else mattered. He belonged to God and his future lay in His hands.

They stopped at Luke's car, and he offered Jeff a new Bible and a hearty handshake.

"You carry around spare Bibles?"

Luke's wide smile spread across his face as he tipped his head. "Sure. Never know who you're going to meet, or where God will lead." He waved as he opened his driver's door. "See you Wednesday. The other men in the study will be glad to have you."

Jeff tucked the Bible under his arm and nodded his response. He sat in his truck for a few minutes. Too grateful to move. He caught a glimpse of his face in the rearview mirror. He didn't know he could smile this big.

He pulled out his phone and texted Jess. He couldn't wait to tell her.

Chapter 39

Jessica's phone whistled, and she read Jeff's text. "Leash the girls and meet me outside. 10 min away."

Well, could he be any more cryptic. What now? At least he didn't show up and ask to come in. What would she do if he kept asking?

Jeff pulled into the drive a few minutes later. He seemed different. He smiled ... fuller? More relaxed? He'd changed.

He took Licorice's leash and her hand and kissed the back of it. They strolled down the street. He didn't say anything for a few minutes. Would he end it today? His behavior rattled her nerves.

"I just came from meeting with Luke." He didn't look at her. His tone hummed with an odd vibration.

"Oh."

"I'll admit, it ticked me off you had him call me."

Every muscle tightened, and she almost missed a step. He hadn't gotten angry with her for being cornered into confessing his past or being taken to the Morgan's, but this upset him?

He clung tight to her hand. "I mean you won't come in my house and won't let me in yours and then you won't even do a Bible study with me. I thought you wished we weren't a couple."

"Oh, no, I—"

"I know, *now*. Luke explained it."

"He did?" How did Luke know—or *what* did he know?

"Yeah, as always you were looking out for us. You wanted to keep our relationship from going too far—from *hooking up*." He winked at her. "I should have figured you would be concerned about our reputations and temptation, and it didn't have anything to do with a lack of interest."

They turned down the next street toward the park. Guilt tickled her. Luke had been exceedingly kind to explain her behavior in such a flattering way, but she had another reason. Well, maybe her actions did cover both purposes. Deep down she knew, not allowing him in her home became another attempt to control the situation. If she kept him out of her place, and never went in his, then when this all ended it wouldn't be as bad to deal with. She wouldn't have all those memories floating around her home like phantoms of what would never be. She'd been protecting *herself*.

"Then Luke asked me to tell him my testimony. I had no idea what he meant. He asked me when I had accepted Christ. Again, I didn't understand. He opened his Bible—"

Jessica jerked to a stop. Licorice pulled his other arm in the opposite direction, and Jeff's body contorted for a moment. "Oh my gosh! I thought—I mean I should have asked—but you said you attended—I assumed—" She took a deep breath, her stomach sour, and her heart heavy as her head hung. She'd never once thought about his faith, too consumed with her own emotions to do more than live through each meeting with him. "I'm sorry."

Without releasing her hand, he reached around her back, pulled her close, and kissed her forehead. "I'm not. I'm glad you never brought it up."

She glanced up not sure how to feel about his comment.

"I've made no secret of the fact I'm crazy about you. I've fallen hard and fast." He shook his head when she opened her mouth. "Whether my reaction is from being alone for such a long time, or because of how amazing you are, or because I saw something in you I desperately needed …" He shrugged. "Probably all of the above. If you had asked me to accept Christ, I would have done it … to make you happy. But today when Luke walked me through the Bible and explained all God had done for me, I knew I wanted what he talked about and, well, it had nothing to do with you. Christ is what I need."

Okay, she was glad she hadn't asked too.

He started them walking again. "I wanted to share the news with someone and you're the only person who matters to me."

"I'm happy for you."

They walked until they came to the same picnic table and snuggled close on the bench. A peace emanated from him. He'd stopped striving, and no urgency simmered under the surface. Jeff stilled.

"I get we need to avoid the temptation for now," he said as he smiled but looked straight ahead.

What did *for now*, mean?

"But we've already broken the rule about not kissing until after."

After what?

"If you want to stop, I'll understand."

Emotion overwhelmed Jessica. A tingle ran over her skin. She reached up and turned his face toward her and pressed her lips to his. A hint of bitterness from his coffee clung to his lips, but their warmth flooded her senses. His always gentle kiss, contained strength and power as well. The smell of hard work and masculinity engulfed her, and she pressed against him to prolong their contact.

His lips turned up in a smile before he withdrew. "I'm glad. I would have missed this."

They sat silently for a long time. "As much as I hate to leave, I need to get to work with the new horse. He has finally allowed me to touch him."

"Me too. I'm almost finished with Shannon's site and about half done with David's. I need to finish them up."

Jeff stood, and they turned back toward her home in silence until they'd almost reached her drive. "Before you ask or get started on it and have a panic attack, I have a huge request. Would you be willing to try and find my girls?"

It had crossed her mind. But she hadn't been able to start, because she didn't know their names. "Okay."

"I'll give you whatever I can, but I don't know where they moved to from Sac or even if they kept my name."

She took both his hands, and their fingers tangled with the leashes. "Lord, You have worked wonders in Jeff's life. As You have restored his life, Jeff desires reconciliation with his daughters. Go before him as he searches and give him wisdom and strength in the process—teach him more of You in the journey. Amen."

"Amen," he said and he claimed her lips again.

Chapter 40

The oppressive heat of August dissipated. A gentle breeze ruffled Jessica's hair. She drew in a deep breath. It seemed like the first in months.

Jeff lay on their picnic blanket on the other side of the small cooler bags and the remnants of lunch. Serenity emanated from him as he lay with his hands laced behind his head, ankles crossed, and eyes closed.

Another deep breath filled her and eased out to join the playful breeze that couldn't seem to decide on a direction to blow.

Storm ambled near Jeff's elbow and munched on the wild grass.

He slid his hand out toward her. She sniffed at it, made one short strong exhale, and resumed her grazing. "Someday, you're going to realize how much you like me, girl."

Jessica smiled.

Two days ago Jeff and Luke had met, and Jeff had given his life to the Lord. He embodied peace now. One of the few puffy clouds sailing above cast a shadow on Jeff's face. Like a watercolor painting, his rugged features softened and smoothed. His head turned toward her and one eye winked open. "You ready?"

Her smile grew as she nodded.

Jeff pushed up and they packed their picnic away. They bumped into each other with their separate stacks of items, and it made Jessica laugh. Once they returned the plates, utensils, and leftovers to the special saddlebag-size picnic coolers, Jeff stood and offered his hand. She grabbed it, rose to her feet, and took the opposite corners of their blanket. He played at not being able to fold it properly, and she giggled.

Blanket stowed away, she offered her hand to him again and he led her as their horses walked beside them.

"I've wanted to show you this ever since the first time you rode Storm."

As they walked, a tiny stone found its way into Jessica shoe. She decided not to stop to deal with it as she strolled with one hand laced with Jeff's and the other leading Storm. It irritated the ball of her foot—much like the secret she fought to keep hidden. She tried to draw from Jeff's peace and ignore both annoyances cutting into her and the pain until it grew unbearable.

A trickle of water increased in volume as they approached. It came into view when they rounded a corner. Between a smattering of evergreens, a waterfall tumbled over a rocky rise about twenty-five feet above them. The mist cast off by the slim stream danced in the sunlight and broke into splashes of rainbows.

Jessica released Jeff's hand to slide her arm around him. She laid her head on his shoulder. "It's beautiful." It would have been a better place for their picnic except for the wet, muddy, or rock-cover ground around the falls.

"You have to see it right at the end of winter. It's gorgeous then. I'm surprised it's flowing at all with as hot as it has been this summer."

Her eyes closed as his comforting strength and the gentle cascade of water lulled her. She didn't want to leave this place—this moment. It had been worth the grief of getting the horses loaded in the trailer. A smile spread again.

Unfortunately, they had to return to the real world. Jessica removed the stone from her shoe before mounting Storm. If she could only get rid of the other irritant as easily. But the secret continued to fester.

Jessica pushed all thought of it aside as they rode back to where the truck and trailer were parked. She took in a deep breath and enjoyed the last of the wild flowers, the tender breeze, and the clouds she imagined formed mythic creatures. She couldn't remember when she'd been this relaxed.

Jessica led her horse in first. The mare didn't resist as long this time.

Jeff took her hand when she exited, and he secured the gate behind Storm. "There's a group from church heading to the river Monday. The last chance to enjoy the summer before everyone heads back to school and the weather cools."

"With it being Labor Day, won't it be crowded?"

"They have a hard to reach, hidden spot closer to Auburn they usually go to. They say not many know about it."

With a near audible crash, Jessica's peace shattered. To say no, would put a wedge between them. To say yes, meant facing her own shame and secrets. When Jeff learned what she'd kept from him all this time, he'd be done with her for sure.

"Come on, it'll be fun."

No, it would be their end.

Chapter 41

Jeff arrived about 10 a.m. A huge picnic basket sat on the center console between them, it symbolized the coming divide in their relationship sure to appear by the end the day. "You all right? You've been too quiet."

"Yeah." The word strained to escape her tight throat.

"If you don't want to go to the river, we can do something else."

Time to face her demons and let Jeff go. It wasn't fair to him to keep secrets when he'd told her his. "No, the river is fine."

Jeff continued to try to draw her into conversation. Her mind wobbled like a wheel snapped from its axle and sent careening across the busy lanes of the highway.

She blinked. They weren't at Discovery Park. "Where are we going?"

"You sure you're okay? We're heading to a swimming hole outside of Auburn."

She remembered—now. Jessica's heart pounded. The long, terrible trip home loomed like a giant monster ready to devour her.

Jeff held the basket with one hand and Jess' with the other as he led her over the rocks. She was troubled. She'd turned pale and become too quiet. She carried the bag with their towels and the blanket to sit on. "You did bring your swimming suit?"

She lifted the hem of her T-shirt to reveal blue and white underneath.

"You can swim?"

Her head jerked up from where she studied the rocky path they tried to navigate. Her brows scrunched together. "Of course."

"Okay. You sure you want to do this?"

Her gaze returned to the obstacles littering their route as she nodded.

They eased down an incline and came to the water's edge. There were a lot of people, many with noisy children. "Let's go downstream a little. I think it's where we'll find everyone."

Her hand quaked in his, but he couldn't tell if the rocks they used as precarious stepping-stones concerned her or if something else bothered her. Jess' bottom lip disappeared between her teeth. Her anxious behavior made his stress level rise.

Jeff took a large step across two stones separated by bubbling water and Jess slipped from his grasp. His head snapped around. She teetered on the rock he'd left as she struggled to keep her balance without his hand and the big tote on her other arm. The bag of towels flew through the air as her arms pin-wheeled, and she fell back with a yelp. She landed on her rump in water up to her chest.

"Jess!"

"I'm all right." She pushed to her feet and water cascaded off her soaked clothes. "I'm also a complete klutz."

Jeff took her hand as she stepped up on the rock he'd moved to and followed him. He led her toward the shore. "I think we have a little farther to go. Why don't you take off the shirt and shorts to let them dry?"

The shirt came off and revealed a modest top of her swimsuit with wide blue straps. She squeezed water out of the tee and tossed it over her shoulder. Jeff couldn't help but smile as he admired her beauty.

"Are we there yet?"

"You're not going to take off the shorts?"

Her face lost all remaining color. Her eyes closed and her rapid breathing told Jeff she fought a panic attack. When she stood from removing her cotton bottoms, Jeff noted the dark blue shorts of her suit and the columns of neat scars on her upper thighs.

She twisted the wet shorts tight in her quaking hands, head down. She flinched when Jeff brushed her shoulder. He slid along her arm until he laced their fingers together. "We all have scars," he said, repeating her words from a few months ago.

He led her a little further before he spotted some faces he knew in a deep pool a few yards ahead but stopped short of joining them. He threw out the blanket on a large flat rock in a bit of sun and pulled her down beside him. With his arm wrapped around her, he drew her close.

She sat rigid, but after a few moments she relaxed into him as always and her head dropped to his shoulder. He kissed the top of it and held her.

He returned a few waves as others from the church noticed them.

"I'm sorry."

He tightened his grip around her. "For what?"

"For never telling you."

"You think I don't understand?"

She pulled away and looked up at him. "I've been terrible to you."

"What?"

"I made you confess your worst shame, cornered you into meeting the Mason's without warning, I've kept you at a distance. Too afraid of my own secrets and shame. I know you must hate me." She covered her face with her hands.

Jeff pulled her shield away and cradled her cheek as he turned her head to look at him. "I love you."

Her flickering gaze searched his face.

"We all have scars," he said again.

Tears pooled in her eyes. "Yes, but you didn't cause yours." He started to open his mouth, but she pulled from him again and shook her head. "Not on purpose." She slid the side of her thumb over the neat columns of identical straight scars. There were about twenty raised white lines in the six columns on each thigh. Every cut measured a half-inch long. The precision spoke of a level of obsession he'd never noticed in her before. She'd been careful to keep the cuts close together so they remained hidden.

"Why come, if you were afraid I'd be mad when I saw you had scars too?"

She wouldn't look at him. "I couldn't bear keeping the secret any longer, but I also couldn't bring myself to tell you." A fatalistic tone etched each word.

"You're still waiting for me to find a reason to make me leave? Do you think so little of me? How could I be put off by your scars when you've readily accepted mine?"

She shook her head. A tear splashed on the white lines and made the smooth skin sparkle. "You deserve better than someone who keeps secrets."

"Then tell me."

She sucked in a ragged breath and coughed.

He lifted her chin and looked in her fear-filled eyes. "Be the woman I know you are. The woman you think I deserve. Be bold."

Her breath stuttered as she tried to inhale.

Chapter 42

Water cascaded over stones in front of them. The breeze swept strands of hair in her face as Jeff sat beside her on a large boulder. Below them, their church family splashed around, and cooked hot dogs and burgers. The savory scent wafted past as Jessica took a deep breath.

Jeff had finally seen her scars. The ones she had cut into her own flesh time and time again. He hadn't left, yelled, or accused. He asked her to tell him about them. "What do you want to know?" she whispered.

"When did you start?"

"High school. I never had many friends, and those I had, didn't last for more than a year or two."

"Why did you start?" He asked a simple question that came with no accusation.

"Control. I couldn't stop the pain I suffered from loneliness. But I could decide when, how often, how deep, and how many cuts. This I could control and in this deliberate act, I had a say as to the pain I would feel."

"When was the last time?"

"A couple of years ago." She absently caressed the final scars she'd added with her thumb. "After high school there were times when I never even considered it. Years went by without adding any or opening old ones." She looked out across the river at the trees that grew between the boulders as they poked out of the hillside. "But when I faced disappointments, rejections, and the loss of my dreams, I'd go through a period where I took up the horrible habit again. When I finally admitted to myself I'd never be married or have children, it happened again."

"Does anyone else know?"

She shook her head. "I've been too ashamed. To have done such damage to myself … what would others say? Especially those in the church."

Her heart skipped a beat as Jeff wrapped his arm around her again and kissed the top of her head. Would she ever be able to accept his continued presence?

"Do you want to leave?" Jeff whispered which drew her into his tender comfort.

Did she? She knew God had forgiven her. She looked toward the familiar faces from church. Would they overlook her failure too?

"We don't have to stay, if you're uncomfortable." He held her tight and it kept her from shattering and falling between the myriad of pebbles around them.

"Maybe it's time to stop hiding?" Had she just asked the question that terrified her most?

His lips pressed to her scalp again. "It did wonders for me. No one judged me for it."

"But yours weren't self-inflicted."

"I think we can both agree our scars have been the result of our poor choices. But we are also forgiven." The tip of his finger brushed over a column of scars with a feather-light caress. "These don't define you. They prove your life hasn't been easy, but God has seen you through."

"When did you get so smart?"

"When God brought you into my life." His finger rose from her leg to under her chin, and he lifted her face. His adoring gaze held her. "And no amount of scars or secrets is going to send me running for the exit. I'm in love with you, and I'm not going anywhere." His lips pressed to hers with such tenderness, her tears started again.

This man could bring her much-hated emotions to the surface faster than anything. If their relationship ever ended, all the cutting in the world wouldn't control the pain.

Jeff's strong loving hand led them to the water's edge. Friends greeted them with smiles. Teens played in the river; adults were gathered around in small groups in patches of sand. A few men added wood to a ring of stones they had created and tried to light it.

Jessica's lungs ached from the breath she held. But when no one gasped, pointed, or accused her, it finally leaked from her tight chest.

David came up and slapped Jeff on the shoulder. "Glad you could make it. We have some hotdogs grilling and there will be s'mores later."

"Thanks. Sounds good." Jeff remained her lifeline and never released her hand.

"The water is perfect," David said as he walked into the river.

Jeff smirked at her. "Yeah, Jess already tested it out for us, with a small slip earlier." Nothing had changed. He stayed beside her, strong, tender, and forgiving. As his glance passed over her once again, her shoulders relaxed and the next breath came easier. The smell of the trees, grilled food, and damp earth, mixed with the sounds of splashed water, and the gentle breeze over her skin to form a blanket of peace around her.

They had a tomorrow. Hope awoke. Could she see beyond one day? Anticipation stretched its wings as it woke again. What would it be like to imagine a life with this amazing man?

Hope wanted to know.

Chapter 43

The sun slipped low on the horizon as Jeff and Jessica climbed into his truck and headed home. She had feared her secret would create an unmovable wall between them, but he accepted her with such love she wanted to be near him. The large center console of his vehicle formed an annoying wall between them now. She couldn't slide close to him, but their fingers sat entwined on top of it.

He squeezed her hand. "Looked like you and Kaitlyn had quite the conversation?"

She rubbed at her scars once again hidden under her shorts. The teen had been one of the few who noticed the many cuts she'd carved into her skin. Jessica didn't want to reveal any confidences. "She understands."

"Good. Then you'll both have support." She marveled at his gentleness and her hateful tears threatened again.

Jessica closed her eyes and tried to ward them off, but even in the darkness behind her lid's, Jeff's love-filled gaze looked at her still. His thumb caressed the back of her hand.

Jess breathed in all he offered her. "I love you." The words came without thought, as easy as a heartbeat. A statement she never dreamed she'd say. The hope growing in her took flight with such force it made her gasp.

Jeff glanced at her, mindful of the busy traffic on the early holiday evening. He raised her hand to his lips and kissed it. "I love you too."

They didn't speak the rest of the way to her house. Jessica bathed in the freedom of her released emotions. They'd been chained a long time

—too long. It felt like a rainbow had burst inside her.

After they pulled in her drive, Jeff leaned over the center console and kissed her. He gazed into her eyes for the longest time before kissing her again. "Thank you."

"For?"

"For choosing to go with me though you were scared, then opening up." He kissed her again. "For loving me—for being you."

Her mind fumbled for non-self-disparaging words to say. All thought vanished away under his consuming stare.

He smiled. "Hey, I know we normally get together on Tuesdays, but can we wait until Thursday? Come over then and bring the girls." His mischievous smirk made her tip her head and scrutinize him.

"The girls?"

"And your laptop."

"All right." He kissed her again before she stepped out of his truck.

Three days later, she leashed the girls and headed to Jeff's. At the end of his house, near the gate to the corral, stood a new white picket fence around one of his sprawling mulberry trees. Jeff's landscape design didn't include lawn, but the space within the fence lay covered in thick new sod. A picnic table sat under the tree. He welcomed her with a kiss as he held open the gate for her.

Licorice jumped up on him while Toffee pulled on the leash to avoid going near him.

"Okay? What have you been up to?"

"Now you can come over anytime and we can work together. At least as long as the weather holds."

She looked around the space. "You went to all this trouble for me?"

"No trouble involved, and it was purely selfish. Now, I can get work done *and* spend time with you." His arm encircled her and she leaned into his strength. "Do you like it?"

"The space and time were very thoughtful."

"But?"

She chuckled. "I usually work in my recliner with my feet up."

"I have a lounge chair somewhere. There's room for it at this end of the table. I think this may work out better anyway. I tend to spread out when I get into a project. Anything else?"

"I have an old laptop. I love it and haven't wanted to upgrade yet, but the battery only lasts a couple of hours."

Jeff paused for a moment and looked back toward his house and sheds. "I can run a power line underground from the shop to right inside the fence and connect it to one of those outdoor power stakes." He kissed her temple. "Have I addressed all your concerns?"

She snuggled against him. "To perfection."

Soon Jessica came to Jeff's almost every day. She'd bring over lunch, or he'd make her something. They'd often work silently for hours in the shade of the mulberry tree, content in one another's presence.

The air developed a nip and Jessica brought a blanket to throw over her lap. They wouldn't be able to work outside like this much longer. The forecast threatened the first rain soon too.

She glanced over at Jeff, as he squinted at his screen. A smile tickled her lips. She knew his dumbfounded look. Some client had asked him to do what they thought would be completely reasonable, but Jeff considered it utterly ridiculous. He would now mull over the need to retain the client against the urge to tell them to forget it. She would miss working beside him every day.

As much as she had embraced their relationship, she still couldn't bear to dream beyond days like this. Moments of quiet togetherness. But hope wanted more.

Jessica closed her laptop. "I think we need to bring in some extra help to find your daughters. I've tried all my tricks, but this is beyond my skill as the names Ammanda and Emmilie Tate aren't as unique as I had thought."

Jeff moved around the table and slumped to the bench closest to her. "And who knows if they even go by Tate anymore." His features were drawn when he glanced up. "Do you think it is even worth it?"

"Do you love them?"

"Of course."

"Miss them?"

"Desperately."

"Don't you think they deserve to know? Even if they aren't ready to rebuild the relationship your ex-wife broke, shouldn't they have the right to make the decision for themselves this time?"

He stood, closed the distance between them, pulled her to her feet, and wrapped her in an embrace. His lips lingered on hers longer than normal. "Do you have someone in mind?"

"There are a few PIs I know. I'll see if any of them are interested and find out how much they'll charge."

"I would love to find them both before Christmas."

"Then we know how we'll pray." Jessica took his hands, and they bowed their heads as she again asked for God's intervention and blessing of the search.

Chapter 44

Rain beat against the office window. Jeff stared at it and stifled the deep urge to curse. It had been months since Jess, and he had worked side-by-side in the oasis he'd created for her and her dogs. The weather had turned fast, and the rain seemed unending this season. Of all years, why did this one have to be a monsoon of torrential downpours? He didn't wish for California to remain in a drought, but seriously … this year?

He leaned back in his desk chair and laced his hands behind his head. The two manila-colored boxes on the shelf in the closet to his right caught his eye. He swiveled and looked at them. Had he filled them over the years for nothing? Would his daughters ever know how much he loved them, or how desperately he missed them every day?

The private eye Jess had worked with hadn't unearthed more than she had yet. Jeff slammed his palms down on the edge of his desk and shoved away from it. He stomped around in a circle, arms behind his head. His line of sight passed the wall of dark bookshelves, followed by the rain-splattered window with its muted light that made his desk gloomier. Again, the neatly organized closet and the two accusing boxes loomed before him and screamed of his failure.

When the door to the room came into view on his second turn, he lunged through it as he tried to escape the whirlwind in his soul. He charged straight down the hall and soon stood in the kitchen. Braced against the counter with rigid arms his head hung low between them, he glanced at his toes.

He straightened and gazed out the window over the sink at the corrals behind his house. With the hard rain, the horses had the good sense to stay in the stables. He could use a little horse sense about now.

He'd been here since shortly after he'd been released from jail. Money from his parent's estate had purchased the land and the rundown home well away from the eyes of the world. He'd lived a quiet life on his tiny ranch with no expectation of ever having more—he never dared hope for it. Jeff had made a good life for himself. He didn't want for anything. With online shopping, he could get all his needs delivered to the house.

He forced his lungs to draw in a slow, deep breath as his eyes closed and his fingers again linked behind his head. Then came the fateful trip to *U Build It* five months ago. Had it only been five months? He took a moment to count them off again. In two days, it would be twenty-four weeks since Jessica Easton had seen him when he'd fought to stay hidden. She'd reached into his dark, secret world and shone God's light powerfully into his soul. Jeff squeezed his eyes closed tighter as if to shield himself from the mighty glow of love she'd brought to his world.

Now, all these weeks later, he behaved like a junkie in need of his next fix. He couldn't quell the cravings he had for her presence. Seeing her a few moments here and there during the week didn't satisfy him. He knew the solution.

But was she ready?

His phone chimed an incoming text from his back pocket. "I'm finally ready." She added a winking emoji and Jeff's heart pounded. "Whenever you are."

Jessica stood next to her car in her driveway when he pulled up a short time later. A box sat on the hood of her vehicle, and she held the girls' leashes tight. He blinked as he realized it had stopped raining. A shaft of light streamed through the clouds and caught in the gold strands of Jess' hair.

Before he got the truck in park, she pulled open the passenger door. Licorice jumped up on the floorboards, onto the seat, over the center console, and into his lap. With her back feet on his thighs and her front paws on his collarbone, she tried to lick him about the face.

"Licorice!" Jess scolded. "Get down."

Jeff looked the dog in the eyes and held her a few inches away to keep out of reach of the lashing tongue. "You'll have to forgive me, Miss Licorice, but there is only one gal I wish to kiss."

Jess sat Toffee on the floorboard and glanced up at him with a smile. "You know her, permission or not, she really doesn't care. I'll warn you again; she has wicked aim."

As if to prove Jess' point, Licorice squirmed and poked her tongue near the corner of his mouth.

"Persistent thing."

"It's your fault for allowing her on your work table, supplying endless belly rubs and treats. Now, she's your friend for life." Jess turned to grab the box from the hood of her car.

Jeff slid out of the truck and left the little black fur-ball on the seat. "Here." He took the box from her. "Hop in and I'll secure this in the bed."

Licorice still stood on his seat when he went to get back in. She didn't greet him with a mere tail wag; the little dog's entire body wiggled.

"Do you plan on driving?"

"Oh, don't tempt her," Jess warned as she tried to get Licorice back over the center console.

Jeff scooped the dog up to keep her out of Jessica's reach.

"She will try to stand on your leg, one front paw on your arm, and the other on the steering wheel, nose on the window."

Jeff tipped his head and raised a brow. "At least one of you knows how to give a proper greeting though."

Jess feigned shock. "Oh, good gracious. Did I forget something?"

Her voice pitched high and airy as she glanced around the cab. The index finger of one hand counted on the digits of her other hand. "Purse. Licorice. Toffee. Box." Her brows crinkled together. "Nope. It's all covered." She turned to him with a smirk. "We're good to go."

Jeff shook his head and laughed. Jess had changed from the woman he met in the parking lot, and even more so since the day at the river when he'd seen the scars she'd cut into her skin. It had been gradual—almost unnoticeable, but when he looked back to those first tentative meetings and compared them to the vibrant, teasing woman who sat beside him now—she had become a different person. Like a flower bud opens to reveal a full bloom.

He leaned toward her. "There is a fare for my taxi services."

She reached for the door handle, mischief dancing in her eyes. "I can always drive."

His head tipped. "Are you going to keep denying me the pleasure of your fine lips?"

She looked at him with radiant joy. "Well, if that's all you want …"

It wasn't. But it would satisfy him for the moment.

With a squirming dog tucked under his arm, he cradled her face to make their contact linger. Oh, how he needed this woman beside him every day.

At last he released her, passed Licorice over, and started the engine. He didn't speak again until they reached the highway. "How much have you told them?"

"What?" Jess settled the dog next to her on the seat.

"How much do your parents know about me?"

She shrugged. "Your jobs, our working together in your yard, going to church together."

"The scars?"

She nodded. "Yeah, I think I mentioned them."

He gripped the wheel a little tighter. "Being a convict."

"What?"

"My time in jail."

"Oh." She looked straight ahead for a while. "I don't think of you as a *convict*. I get you made a mistake, but you never meant to hurt anyone. You never tried to get a lighter sentence. You paid for your mistake and have worked hard to never put anyone else in danger like that again. Then you hid yourself away for years, to further serve a penance for your wrong deeds. As far as the Morgan's and the law are concerned, you've more than paid your dues."

"Your parents don't know then?"

"Maybe. I can't remember."

"Well then this could be an interesting Thanksgiving."

"You don't have to tell them."

Yes, he did. Jeff needed to have a conversation with her father before the day concluded. He had no intention of starting it out by deceiving the man.

Chapter 45

Jeff drove with his left hand and laced the fingers of his right with hers. Jess' thumb tapped in rhythm with the worship songs on the radio. He caught her singing along a few times—though no louder than a whisper. Licorice squeezed next to her on the seat and Toffee curled at Jess' feet. His railing emotions from earlier in the morning settled. Her presence impacted him in such positive ways. Excitement stirred in him any time they were together. It surprised him though when she rested back in the seat and let her eyes droop closed now and then. People were usually more nervous when introducing their parents to the person they're dating.

The early rainy morning had turned into streams of sunlight through the smattering of clouds now. The temperature hadn't risen above fifty degrees, though. The truck's heater kept the chill at bay, but did nothing to sooth his nervousness. If everything went as planned, today would consist of more than meeting her parents and making a good impression. Jeff drew in a slow deep breath and released it. About fifty minutes from Jess' house, they drove through the foothills above Sacramento. The next few hours would determine the directions of his future—his happiness—his entire life. One more deep calming breath.

Once off the highway, they moved along many streets until Jess had them turn onto a twisting lane lined with black oaks. Around one last bend a house came into view. Other than being blue, it reminded him a lot of his place. Both structures where long ranch style homes, but this one had a large porch out front.

Jess directed him where to park. There were a lot of cars in the yard, an old Plymouth, a Blazer, a newer Oldsmobile, and at least two more covered up at the side of the house. Hadn't she said they would be the only ones here besides her parents?

Licorice sprang into his lap as he cut the engine while Toffee jumped on the seat with Jess. "It's best to let them out before they have a fit. They'll go straight for the house."

He opened the door and the little black dog sprang to the ground and vanished. Toffee danced on the other side and made half-hearted attempts at jumping over the console into his lap but never committed. He stepped out of the truck, and she dashed past him. He turned and looked at Jess with a raised brow.

She had already stepped out and now moved to the bed to retrieve the box of items she had brought.

Jeff handed her a bundle of flowers before he collected her larger item.

She refused to take it. "Oh, no. If those are for Mom, you have to give them to her. She'll never believe I didn't get them for you to give to her."

He hesitated for a moment, but Jess snatched up what she had brought and headed for the front door.

"Should I have brought a dish to share too?"

She smirked over her shoulder. "You brought me—and the girls. You've done more than enough."

Jeff followed her through the front door and the long living room. A fire glowed in the fireplace at the opposite end. They turned to the right before they reached it. An octagon table sat covered in a blue tablecloth, the blue and white plates and cobalt glasses already in place. "We're here," Jess said as she sat the box on the bar dividing the dining area from the kitchen proper.

"Hey, hon."

Jeff hadn't known what to expect of her parents, but the woman coming toward him wasn't it. Only her salt and pepper hair and slightly wrinkled skin marked her as being older than Jess. Brown eyes smiled at him as much as her pink lips. Her movements were spry and easy as she hugged her daughter and then gave him one too. Her arms were strong, and he felt no tremor in her hold.

"I'm glad you could make it. Nothing fancy, just the basics."

"Thank you, Mrs. Easton. It smells amazing." He offered her the flowers.

"Well, aren't you sweet. Call me Carol." As Jess' mother turned toward the sink with the flowers, a man stepped through the sliding glass door in front of them. Toffee barked until she howled.

"It really isn't me." Jeff said with a chuckle.

"Nope, she really dislikes men." Carol smiled.

The man stood a little taller than Jess. She slipped into his arms and tucked her head under his chin. The sleeves of his lightweight jacket were pushed up to reveal muscles beneath tanned skin. Again, only his white hair marked his age. Jeff tried to do some quick calculations. If they'd had Jess when they were twenty, they had to be in their seventies. But it didn't seem possible. Jeff's mother had passed in her late fifties and even before her illness, she'd been bent, quaked when she stood, and weak all over. These two didn't look or act much older than Jess and he did.

Mr. Easton reached out a hand; it was rough and calloused like his own. "Glad you're here. I'd had hoped to get the firewood in before you arrived, but the rain hung me up. I'll be back in a minute and then get cleaned up."

Jeff glanced at Mr. Easton's torn jeans brushed with dust and a faded shirt peeked out from the jacket. "I'll help you."

"No you won't." Both Jess' parents spoke at the same time.

"You're the guest," Carol said.

"I'll only be a couple of minutes," Mr. Easton added.

"Still, I'd like to help."

Jess waved her hand at her father. "You might as well let him, Dad. He's using the tone he does when he means to come with you whether you invite him or not." She flashed Jeff a smile and moved to help her mother.

After a moment's hesitation, they stepped outside and Mr. Easton grabbed the wheelbarrow parked next to the back door. He maneuvered it around the house to the far end of the property.

All manner of plants filled the yard; a black oak with a deck around it, a bare walnut tree with bands of colored rocks beneath it, pines and cypress on the slope, and a meandering lawn. Stone paths led from the cement patio to several areas under empty canopy frames. "You have a lovely yard."

"Thank you. It's a challenge to keep up, but we enjoy it in the spring and summer."

They came to an area littered with wood, two whole trees lay next to each other, a pile of sawdust sat between several cut rounds, and an ax leaned against a stump with a wedge on top. Surely, he didn't still split wood at his age.

Mr. Easton reached to the neat stack of wedges of oak and alder and filled the wheelbarrow.

Jeff did likewise. "I'm completely in love with your daughter," he blurted as Mr. Easton bent to grasp the handles of the wheelbarrow.

Jess' father stood and glanced at him, one white brow rose high.

"I know I don't deserve her."

Chapter 46

Mr. Easton stood straighter still and his face pinched as he considered Jeff. "What an odd thing to say."

"I can't imagine my life without her."

"Well, she's happier than I've ever seen her."

Jeff took a deep breath and pushed up his sleeve revealing his scarred arm. "I did a terrible thing a few years back, and I spent time in jail because of it. I'll completely understand if you don't want your daughter involved with a criminal, but I have to say I don't know what I'd do without her."

"This might be easier if you start at the beginning," Mr. Easton said with a kind smile.

Jeff told Jess' father his entire story: his poor marriage, the fight, the car accident, jail time, and his self-imposed exile from society. Mr. Easton's expression never changed. He continued to stare expressionless at Jeff. Why didn't the man say something? What was he thinking?

"Jess saw me when no one else ever did. She never shied from my scars," Jeff said to finish.

Mr. Easton smiled. He unzipped his jacket and undid a couple of buttons of his shirt to reveal his left shoulder to Jeff. Irregular patches of smooth white covered his skin—the evidence of grafts. "Scars wouldn't bother her. An accident on the job when she was a toddler left me with these. She doesn't remember me before the accident."

"She has said, more than once, 'we all have scars.'"

Mr. Easton patted Jeff's shoulder, "True." He zipped his jacket up with a shiver. "Let's get this back to the house before we both freeze.

The ladies will wonder what is taking us so long."

"Can't I do anything to help?"

"No, I've got it."

"I'd be happy to, but I came out here with you for another reason."

Mr. Easton straightened once more. By his lopsided smile, he knew what Jeff wanted to ask. But Mr. Easton waited for him to say the words.

"Now that you know my past, would you still give me your blessing to ask Jess to marry me? I know were both mature adults, but you are important to Jess, and I don't want to do anything to hurt her relationship with you or her mother."

"My girl has a mind of her own."

Jeff dug his boot into the soft soil and laughed. "I've noticed."

"The Lord has forgiven a great many failings in my past. I can't hold your mistakes against you. If she is agreeable, I'd welcome you into the family." Mr. Easton offered his hand again.

"Thank you, sir."

"Now, if we're going to be family, you have to call me Rob." He raised a bushy white brow again. "And, if there is nothing else, I'd like to get back inside before my old bones turn to ice."

Jeff stepped out of the way and the wheelbarrow rolled past him with a speed Jeff thought he would have trouble maintaining. He caught up and walked beside Rob as they headed for the house.

"When do you plan to pop the question?"

"Not sure Jess is ready, and I'd like to find my daughters first … Soon, though. I've waited long enough to find her. I'll let you know."

"Make sure Carol and you trade numbers before you leave."

With the wheelbarrow returned to its place next to the door, Rob picked up two pieces of wood and pulled the slider open for Jeff to reenter the kitchen. Toffee howled at them both.

You better decide I'm your friend, little girl. We're going to be family soon if this works out like I'm praying.

"Well you seemed to have a good time." Jess had the sassy smirk again as they drove back down the highway.

"Your parents are great. Why wouldn't I have had a great time?"

"I know you and Dad hit it off." She chuckled. "But you ignored Mom and me."

"I did not." Jeff took a moment to remember the afternoon around the Thanksgiving table. The amazing food. He'd never had a smoked turkey before, but he preferred it over a deep-fried bird now. All the fixings were good too. But nothing had compared to the stories her dad told or his laughter at Jeff's tales. Then there had been the competitive game of Yahtzee. He couldn't remember the last time he'd played any game not on his computer.

As he considered the afternoon closer, it occurred to him Jess was right. "Sorry," he said glancing at her, "didn't mean to neglect you."

She laughed. "I haven't seen Dad have such a good time in a while. I'm thrilled it went well."

"Me too." Jeff said it more to himself. Jess had no idea how well the day had gone.

Jeff settled into his chair, clicked on the computer, and scrolled through his email.

The name of the investigator Jess had connected him with caught his eye. "Hey Jeff, Sorry the search has taken so long. I'm pretty sure I've located Ammanda. I'll call you after the holidays. Have a great one."

His baby—well she would be nineteen now. She'd been two last he saw her. How would she feel about him reaching out? Would they ever have the relationship Jess had with her father? *Lord* ... He didn't know how to finish his request.

Chapter 47

Jeff fidgeted in his seat again.

Jess tightened her fingers with his. "Do you need to pull into the next rest stop?"

"No." There weren't any on Highway 99 anyway, but it didn't matter because he didn't need a bathroom. He squirmed again.

"Need to stop and walk around?"

"No. I just want to get there and get it over with. Can't believe they grew up only three hours away."

"I can't believe it took Ammanda over two months to get back to you. Any word from your other daughter?"

"No." His chest tightened until it hurt for Jeff to draw in a breath. He clicked the wipers up to a higher speed to deal with the heavier rain. "Do you think I'm doing the right thing?" His decision to meet his daughter had been worse than the choice to go to church with Jess the first time. Harder than when he thought Jess intended to break off their relationship after he'd told her he loved her.

Jeff adored being a father. He loved his daughters. But he'd missed too much. The many memories, birthdays, special performances at school or maybe they were into sports. He could almost picture Emmilie racing down the field after a soccer ball. But he didn't know if she'd ever played.

The most crucial growing and developing years were gone and impossible for him to get back now. Could it be too late?

Jess raised his hand she held and kissed the back of it, and it jerked him from his terrified thoughts. "Do we need to pray again?"

"Not while I'm driving. I want to concentrate on the words when we pray. Right now, I can't think." He saw a water-streaked blur of green as they passed a distance sign. "Did you see that? How far did it say to Fresno? I didn't see it." Jeff cleared his throat of the panic giving his words an edge. The temperature outside his truck on this mid-January day barely registered over forty degrees. The morning's light drizzle that had turned in to heavy sheets didn't help his mood either. Even with the dismal weather, nervous sweat made his shirt stick to him. What if his scars disgusted Ammanda like they had her mother? What if …

"About an hour." Jess squeezed his hand again.

An hour. It might as well be an eternity. He'd waited almost nineteen years to find them. Then weeks for Ammanda to respond. Now this horrendous drive in the pouring rain.

Jeff's thumb drummed on the steering wheel. He hated traveling 99. One lane over some stretches and stops in small towns. Even out on the larger two-lane areas, too many vehicles entered and exited the highway to maintain the speed limit or any consistent speed. He glanced at the time again.

"We'll be there almost an hour before she agreed to meet you." Jess kissed his hand again. "Why don't you pull over?"

He needed to get there faster, not stop. "I'll be all right. What if they hate me?"

"Has God failed you yet?"

"No." Jeff released the word more as a defeated sigh than an affirmation of how good God had been to him.

"Tell me what He has already done for you?"

"Why? You know my story. You've lived much of it with me."

"Because we all need standing stones."

Jeff glanced at her with a raised brow, then returned his gaze to the road.

"Often, when God preformed a miracle for His people—like when

He parted the Red Sea, the Jordan River, gave them a victory, whatever
—they gathered stones and stacked them up to make a memorial. Then
when they saw the standing stones again, they were reminded of God's
faithfulness. When their children asked why the stones stood there, they
would teach them about how God took such good care of them."

Jeff nodded. "Well, He gave me you." He squeezed her hand this
time and pulled it up to kiss.

"Even before we met."

"Before? He … He didn't let Malcolm and Wanda die."

"And?"

"And … they forgave me and prayed for me."

"And?"

What did he miss? What else had God done? Jess didn't clue him in.
He would have to come up with it on his own. His thoughts scattered—
like swatting at flies on a hot summer day in the barn, he missed more
than he got. "He saved me." Jeff said in a whisper.

"The day of your accident, and later for eternity."

The next breath came easier. God had saved him. He sat here now,
on his way to see his daughter, because of everything God had done for
him when He hadn't been looking for God. The thought took root.
Before Jeff knew or acknowledged God, his Heavenly Father had been
at work to change his life. They could have been anyone, but he'd
crashed into a family who trusted God. He needed to do it now too.
Trust God.

"You have no control over how your daughters will respond to you
reaching out to reconnect. You have let them know you love them, but
they may not accept what you offer them. Personally, I think they will,
but only God knows for sure. But let's say Ammanda doesn't respond
well when you meet her today. Will her rejection change your salvation in
Christ?"

"No." He said it with a great deal more confidence this time.

"Will it change how much He loves you?"

"No." Jeff smiled and kissed her hand again. "And I know it won't change anything between us either. In fact, nothing will change. Though I want to reconnect with them, if they refuse—either or both of my daughters—nothing at all will change for me." His shoulders lost some of their tension and his neck its stiffness.

"Good. Now you can trust God for whatever happens."

"But I still hope you're right. I want them in my life."

"We have prayed for reconciliation."

Chapter 48

They sat in front of the place Ammanda had instant messaged him about and prayed off and on for almost forty-five minutes. He didn't have her number—only a social media account to connect with her.

Jess walked inside the coffee shop with him before the appointed time. He sat at a table where he faced the entrance. His leg bounced, and he startled with every jingle of the bell over the door. Jess waited at another table closer to the wall and though she faced him, her bowed head told him she continued to pray.

Their meeting time came and went. Five minutes, then ten. How long did he wait for her? Forever seemed a bit impractical. Who'd feed the horses? *Breathe, Jeff. Just breathe.* He tried to recall the words to the worship song by the same name. They wouldn't come. *Trust God.*

A young woman entered. She wore tight dark jeans, red checkered sneakers, her belly peeked out of a striped shirt, and over it a long, baggy, gray sweater. Her light strawberry blond hair fell past her shoulders now, but she still had bangs. But in her eyes, he saw the shadow of his little girl in the woman who approached him.

She didn't smile or greet him as she pulled out the chair on the opposite side of the table, and dropped into it. She sat on the edge of her seat. The thin strap of her purse remained on her shoulder as if she would bolt at any moment.

"Can I get you anything—"

"No."

Jeff eased back down in his own chair. "Thank you for coming."

"Whatever. It won't make any difference."

Jeff took a breath to steady his nerves and dared a glance at Jess. She smiled back and lowered her head again. He gazed at Ammanda's lovely features. "You are beautiful."

"I take after Mom."

Jeff smiled. "I'm glad."

She stared at him.

How different his meeting with strangers had been. People he'd wronged had welcomed him instantly. Now, he sat with his flesh and blood, and she would barely speak to him. Did she hate him, or was this her normal demeanor? "I've missed you."

"Then you shouldn't have bailed on us."

Lighting flashed in the window behind her and the down pour from earlier returned.

"What?" He hadn't expected to be blamed for leaving.

She sat her forearms on the table and leaned toward him. Her words flew, louder than he wished. "You ran out, leaving us with nothing. To make ends meet, Mom brought home one loser after another. I've had five daddies, each one worse than the last. But it seems she has always had terrible taste in men."

"Mandy—"

Her fist slammed on the table. "Don't call me that!"

Jeff swallowed. "Ammanda, I didn't leave."

"Of course you did. One day you were there and then you vanished."

He undid the buttons on his right sleeve cuff and pushed up the fabric. "I caused an accident. I spent months in the hospital. Then I went to jail for a year. When I got out, I went to our home but my key didn't work and a stranger answered the door. You, Emmilie, and your mom were gone. My house had been sold, and I didn't know where you were."

She burst from her chair and it scraped across the tiles. "You're lying!"

He stood and reached out a hand toward her. "Ammanda …"

She shook and stared with wide eyes as she jerked away from him.

Jeff remembered the fright in her eyes. She'd looked at him the same way the first time he tossed her in the air and caught her. Emmilie had loved it as a toddler. Ammanda … not as much.

Her head shook back and forth, but her words were quiet and strained. "No, you're lying. You have to be lying."

"Please, Ammanda, sit. Let's talk about it."

She stepped away from him. "No. You're lying." She whirled and ran out the door into the pouring rain.

Chapter 49

Jeff stepped to race after his fleeing daughter. He hadn't seen her in sixteen years and in their three-minute meeting, she'd accused him of abandoning her, called him a liar, and had run away.

A hand took hold of his arm and stopped him. "Let her go," Jess whispered. She wrapped him in a tight hug. "She came to pick a fight, not hear the truth. Let what you told her sink in before you try again."

She released him and Jeff dropped back into his chair. He thought reconnecting might be difficult, but he'd never imagined their reunion could go this terrible. His wife stole his children and had somehow made his youngest daughter believe he had been in the wrong.

Jess moved the box he'd brought for Ammanda onto the table and took the chair beside him. He couldn't catch a full breath and he ached like he'd been punched in the gut. He barely registered as Jess took both of his hands in hers. She held tight as her head bowed again. "Heavenly Father, You know the pain of loving Your children who spurn your affection. Shower Your comfort on Your son right now. Ease his heartache. Reveal the truth to Ammanda. Bring the lies into the light and lay them bare where they can do no more harm. Intervene in this relationship, Lord. Make right the connections ripped apart in spite and hate. Rebuild the trust and love between these lost girls and their father. We ask all this in Your name. Amen."

"Amen," Jeff whispered. Her prayer had taken the worst of the sting out of his daughter's rejection, but he still hurt. A single tear escaped. When he opened his eyes, Jess smiled at him.

"Remember what Jesus told His disciples, 'In the world you will have tribulation. But take heart; I have overcome the world.' And this story isn't finished yet. You've had it pretty easy thus far. Now you'll need to stretch your faith muscles a little."

"I hate exercising," Jeff said as he leaned and tipped his head against hers.

She laughed and kissed him. "Come on. I'm starved. There has to be some place different to eat around here than what we have in Sac." She stood and collected Ammanda's box and Jeff felt the prick of his daughter's rejection afresh.

You have overcome the world, God. You can prevail with one misinformed young woman too. I will trust in You. He looped his arm around Jess, and they stepped out onto the sidewalk. "Good grief, it's still coming down in sheets. I didn't think it rained like this here."

"God is crying with you." Jess rested her head on his shoulder. She always knew the right thing to say.

"I'll get the truck—"

She shook her head. "Let's run together and each get on our phones to look for a restaurant. Give the rain a bit longer to let up. I hate being on the road when it's coming down this hard. Can't see a thing."

They agreed, took a deep breath, and raced hand in hand to the vehicle. They were soaked when they got inside. "It's crazy out there," Jeff said and reached for anything they could use to dry off a little.

"Hope it lets up soon or we'll float away."

They'd found a Chinese buffet a few blocks away and were finishing their meal when Jeff's phone chimed an incoming text. As usual, he didn't look at it. Jess loved how he focused and always gave her his full attention. But something nudged at her. "Why don't you check the message?"

"Well, you're with me, so it has to be work. I'll get to it tomorrow. We have the drive home." He glanced behind her out the windows of the restaurant. "Rain looks like it's stopped. You ready?"

She shook her head and crossed her arms. "Just look."

He sighed but pulled his phone from his pocket. His eyes opened wide. "I think it's Ammanda."

Excitement bubbled in her, and Jess leaned on the table. "I thought you didn't have her number."

"I don't—or didn't—but I gave her mine one of the first times I emailed her."

"What'd she say?" Jess leaned over, and stretched to see the screen.

"You still in town?" Jeff glanced up. "It has to be her, right? It looks like a Fresno number, and it's not in my contacts. Do you think it's her?"

Jess snatched the phone from him, typed "Ammanda?" and hit send before handing it back.

They held their breath. A minute later the phone dinged again and Jess slid out of her side of the booth and made Jeff scoot over and sat beside him.

"Yes. Are you still in town?"

"We're at a Chinese buffet near the coffee shop. Do you want to meet again?" Jeff hit send. "Please," he whispered.

Jess kept her eyes on the text feed. "She didn't know you were with anyone, I might freak her out."

A new text popped up. "K."

The phone shook in Jeff's hands. "Okay? What does she mean?"

Before he could respond, a new text appeared. "B there in a few."

Jeff squeezed Jess' arm until her fingers tingled. "She's coming here?" He stared. "What do I say to her? How do I help her understand?"

Jess took a slow breath, rested her hand on his cheek, and kissed him. "First, we pray for wisdom. Then when she gets here, listen. She might have a lot to say to you. You don't have to worry about what you'll say. The Holy Spirit will guide you in all your ways."

Chapter 50

Jess tried to leave, but Jeff made her slide deeper into the booth and trapped her between him and the wall. His knee bounced as he watched the door with unblinking eyes. He fought to inhale but his tight chest wouldn't expand to let it in.

Finally, Ammanda entered. Her gaze scanned the room to find him. She took tentative steps and dragged her toes across the floor.

Jeff jumped up. His thigh hit the table. A nerve grating noise disturbed the serene room as it scraped over the floor.

Ammanda startled.

"Thank you for coming," Jeff managed to mumble. He waved for her to sit across from them and straightened the table, with another ear-piercing grate.

Without moving, Ammanda stared at Jess.

"This is my girlfriend, Jess … Jessica Easton."

"Oh," she continued to stare as she flopped into the opposite side of the booth. Then she looked at her lap. The silence choked the life out of the room.

Jess held his hand and jerked it every time he started to open his mouth.

"I called Em after I left." She looked up at Jeff. Red and puffy eyelids drew attention to her bloodshot eyes. "She said you told the truth." She grabbed a napkin and wiped her nose. "Em was eight, last time we saw you. She says she remembers overhearing mom talk to Aunt Sue and some of her friends. She said; 'I can't believe he has done this to me,' and 'I'm mortified. How can I show my face here any longer? I'm just going to have to move and leave everything behind.' So, she left. Mom abandoned you and told me it was all your fault. You just walked out on us." She sniffed again.

"I've never really talked about it with Em. I was mad at *you*, and I didn't want to hear mom had been in the wrong. Em could have tried harder, but mom and I were close and she has always blamed you for leaving. But Em could have said …" Her words faded.

"I'm sorry."

"Why are you sorry? You didn't lie to me my entire life. Why'd mom do it? Em and mom should have told me the truth?" She hiccupped through more tears. "Why'd it have to be this way?"

"Ultimately, I caused it all when I drank too much. I did a horrible thing and got behind the wheel of my car and caused the serious accident."

"But …"—she dabbed at her nose again and brushed away new tears—"she took us from you without saying a word where we were going. She *lied* to me."

"I don't blame your mother, Ammanda. She did what she thought best to protect you girls and bring you up in a safe environment."

"Safe?" Ammanda snorted. "Well, she failed there."

Jeff choked on his next thought. "None of your step-fathers …" He couldn't finish his sentence.

She waved her hand, which held the now soggy napkin. "No, thank God. They yelled. One locked us in our room a lot. We heard the constant fighting. We'd move out into tiny one-room apartments, have to change schools, and not get enough to eat. Until Mom found a new guy. We'd move into his house, change schools again, and deal with his failings until mom got tired of him and it started all over again. She married some, but thankfully not all of them."

"I am sorry, Ammanda. If I could change what I did then, I would."

She shrugged and stared at the table. "Not much we can do about it now."

Jeff let go of Jess' hand for a moment and picked up her box he'd retrieved from the truck. He placed it on the table and slid it across to Amanda. "I can't fix what I broke. But I wanted you to know how very much I love you."

"What's this?"

"It's yours."

Ammanda stared at it for a moment before she lifted off the lid and took the first folded paper inside. Jeff had never reread anything he placed in the box. The first time he wrote these notes and letters had held enough pain—he hadn't wanted to relive it by reading them again. He'd added each message behind the last he'd wrote, and he knew the one she held from the front of the box he had written while in jail. He apologized for being such a terrible dad in it. Next, she pulled out the first homemade card he'd made for her third birthday, followed by the one for her fourth. By the time her fifth birthday, he been released from jail, and he knew their mother had taken them away. But he bought her a card anyway, and wrote her a long note about how much he missed her and hoped to see her again soon. Then he'd tucked five dollars inside.

Ammanda held the money in one hand. Jess passed her another napkin she took without looking up. She blew her nose. Her eyes scanned the remaining notes and cards still contained in the box.

"There hasn't been a single day I haven't thought about you and wished I could be with you to hold you and hear about the details of your life."

Chapter 51

Jeff sat across the table from his youngest daughter as she picked through the messages he'd written her in the time they'd been apart. He reached in the back of the box and pulled out a bank deposit book tucked there. "Several years ago, I talked to an attorney, and we calculated how much I should have paid in child support. I put the sum we figured and a little more when I had it in to an account. Think of it as a college fund." He handed her the book.

She opened it and her eyes went wide. She coughed and covered her mouth with the napkins. "Are you serious? This is Em' and mine?"

"No. This is yours. I have a similar box of letters and cards and a separate college account for your sister."

Ammanda slid out another card and stared at him. "These birthday cards?"

"All have money in them too."

Her finger brushed over the years of messages poured from his heart, filled with all the love he could put into words, and sprinkled with a little money here and there totaling about two hundred dollars not including the college account.

Her sniffles increased as she continued to stare and brush the papers with her fingers. She whispered mournful words. "All these years I wanted a proper dad, while my dad wanted me."

"Yes, I did and do. I love you, Ammanda."

With tears streaming down her face, she looked up at him. "Daddy."

He wiped his hand across his wet cheeks and grinned, "Mandi-girl."

She tucked her hair behind her ear and showed him a slim smile.

"Where we go from here is up to you. But know I am always here for you and your sister."

"I wish I'd known about this sooner." She waved the bank book. "Em graduated midterm from a college in Missouri last month. Mom and I couldn't afford to go celebrate with her." She shook the book again. "If we'd only known."

"You don't have to dip into your college fund, I can pay for you to go visit."

Amanda shook her head. "Graduation's over and she's all packed up ready to come back to California as soon as the weather is good. She hates driving in the snow and ice. She can be a dietitian anywhere. Where better than in SoCal where everyone wants to be skinny and healthy."

Ammanda's phone made a musical sound. She glanced at it and groaned. She put the notes and cards back in the box. "I have to head home. I told mom I'd help her with some stuff before I went to work later." Her hand caressed the top of the box as she looked up at Jeff again. "I don't want to see her right now let-alone help her. I'm furious. How stupid could she be to leave you and to keep us apart?"

"Don't be too hard on her."

"How can you go easy on her? If you really love us as much as these letters seem to say, how can you not be mad at her for all the time we lost?"

"Because I blame myself too. I've spent a lot of years being mad at myself. But I have been forgiven and have finally learned to forgive myself. I hope one day you and Emmilie can forgive me too."

Ammanda again stared at the box and rubbed her hands over it. "Em wants you to come to her welcome home party when she gets back."

"I would love to come if it won't upset your mother too much."

"Who cares if she's upset. She kept us apart all these years because of how she thought others viewed *her*. She didn't care about what your absence would do to me—or even you. If Mom doesn't want you there, *she* can leave. Em wants you there. I want you there."

Ammanda stood and Jeff followed.

"You'll come, right?"

"I will for you Mandie-girl."

They looked at one another. Jeff reached out a hand toward her. She didn't take it but slipped close for the most awkward hug he'd ever experience. Weak. Sloppy. Not particularly warm. "I'll let you know when we have a date for the party."

"Sounds good."

She picked up her box and cradled it to her chest. "Bye, Daddy."

"Bye, sweetheart. Let me know if you need anything."

She had turned to the door but nodded without looking back.

Jeff dropped down beside Jess. He put his elbows on the table and his face in his hands. The tears came hard now.

Jess linked her arm with his. "Thank You, gracious Father for Your loving kindness …" Her words dissolved into tears as well.

Chapter 52

Jeff needed this time with Jess. He had to admit, sitting outside in temperatures in the mid-fifties might be uncomfortable. She sat on the lounge chair beside the picnic table in his side yard.

Though the warmest day of the year so far, this early March day held no real heat. Covered in a blanket, wearing fingerless gloves, a heavy sweatshirt, and a knit cap, Jess looked ready for a trek in the snow not a day working beside him in his yard.

He added another log to the outdoor firepit between them and rubbed his hands together. He ignored the cool temperature and frequent breeze disrupting his papers, because he would take this day over any of the long days of winter where he worked inside alone. They needed to be married.

His phone dinged with an incoming text.

"Ammanda again?" A lump under the blanket at Jess' feet moved as she looked over at him. Both her dogs jostled beneath the covering.

"Yep."

"Saturday, right?"

"Yes, according to Ammanda, Emmilie should be in Fresno tomorrow. She'll have a couple days to rest up and then the party. You sure you won't go with me?"

"For one, I haven't been invited. Secondly, your daughter has made her wishes pretty clear."

Jeff knew Ammanda wished he'd get back together with her mother, which he didn't want. But something continued to prevent him from asking Jess to marry him. Hopefully, by Saturday evening when he headed home, he'd feel free to ask her the critical question.

He took a moment to scan the message from his daughter. They hadn't seen each other or talked—except through texts—since they'd met in January. He believed if he mattered to her as she seemed to write, there would be more than these infrequent messages between them.

Saturday hit him like a tsunami wave. Jeff braced his arms against the dresser and let his head hang. Air wheezed into his chest. His heart beat an erratic rhythm. He tried to straighten but his stomach tightened too much to accomplish it. He tugged on his right shirt cuff and fought to make his collar stand taller. Why try to hide the scars? Ammanda had seen some of them and didn't freak out. Would Emmilie be bothered by them? Molly. She'd had issues merely looking at the bandages covering the wounds. Would she be repelled by his scars now? Why did it matter?

He braced himself against the dresser again. His limbs shook. *I haven't had a panic attack—not since Jess … Jess.* Oh, he loved her, and it shouldn't matter a wit what Molly thought of him. Not anymore. Shame no longer had a hold on him. God had set him free.

Jeff's knees gave way, and he dropped to the carpet—thankful he hadn't gotten around to switching it out for hardwood floors yet. "Lord, I have been forgiven—by You and the Morgans. I am a new creation in You. Fear, shame, and dread are no longer a part of my life. I am free." His next few breaths came easier. Pastor Matt had preached about using Scripture when in trouble, like Jesus did when Satan tempted him in the desert. None would come to mind right away. He locked his arms straight and braced them on his knees as he sat back on his heels.

"Even though I walk through the valley of the shadow of death, I will fear no evil, for You are with me." The words slid off his lips from deep within his soul. The one verse he'd learned as a child from the twenty-third chapter of Psalms. No, a visit to Molly couldn't be considered the valley of the shadow of death, but dread still threatened to overtake him. "I don't know why this visit is getting to me like this, Lord. I want to see my girls and be a part of their lives. But I don't want to go back. I want to move forward. Forward with Jess and with You. Lord be with me today."

The tension leaked out of him with his next breath. Jeff sat still and quiet in the following moments. Whatever the day brought; it would be all right because God would be part of it. *How did I ever manage before I had God in my life?*

Later in the day, nerves threatened to stop Jeff, but he drove to the girls' home despite them. The door opened to laughter and a young woman with long blonde hair turned from whomever she'd been joking with to greet the newcomer. The smile faded instantly when her gaze fell on Jeff. Her light eyes lost their merriment. "Hey."

"Hello, Emmilie. It's good to see you."

"Yeah." Her gaze slid from his face to the box tucked under his arm. "That for me?" Her brows rose.

"Yes."

She snatched it from him before he could say more. "Thanks." She called over her shoulder as she walked into the house and left him outside without an invitation to come in.

Chapter 53

Jeff stood on the doorstep of his ex-wife's home. He'd been told that his oldest daughter wanted him to come and celebrate her return to California after graduating from college. Emmilie had given him the barest of greeting before taking her box of cards and notes.

"Dad!" Ammanda, his youngest, bounded toward him. "You're finally here." She waved him inside and closed the door behind him. "Mom's in the kitchen. Come on."

She made no attempt to greet him—no hug. Without further comment, she walked to the back of the house. On the right sat a small dining table with spindly, dented legs. Chipped stain marred the wood. It looked to lean a bit to one side, and it appeared the dingy cream wall held it upright. Three white plastic chairs awaited occupants. An old-style hanging light with its multiple rectangles of smoky glass hung from the ceiling not quite centered above the table.

To his left, a bar covered in stained Formica countertop added to the neglected kitchen. Two miss-matched barstools, about the same vintage as the rest of the furniture, stood in front of the bar.

"Dad's here," Ammanda announced with such excitement she almost bounced.

Molly turned with a small smile as she pulled a sheet of cookies from the oven. They were lumpy and misshapen and darker than Jeff preferred. "Well, hello." Her gaze ran over what she could see of him from behind the bar. "You've aged fairly well."

"Thanks. You look good." He lied. She must have gained at least forty pounds which did her stunted frame no favors. Could it be that the added weight actually made her look shorter? She couldn't be over four and a half feet though in his memory she had seemed taller. Her hair was cut so it only came to her chin, and she styled it around her face. It made her head look like a large bowling ball with her eyes and nose being the finger holes. It was blonder than he remembered.

Molly tossed out a hip and flipped her hair. "I've got good genes, and"—her gaze roamed over his scars—"I've taken good care of myself."

He heard the familiar dig in her tone, but it didn't prick his emotions as he'd expected it to. *Thank You, Lord.* "I appreciate you allowing me to come," he worked to change the subject.

She pried the cookies off the sheet and waved the spatula at him dismissively between dropping the crunchy chunks of hard dough onto a plate. "Well of course. She's your daughter too. It's good you've reached out. I know it has meant a lot to Mandi."

Jeff glanced around for Ammanda, but she'd vanished. Molly picked up the plate and waved for him to follow as she stole a glimpse at his right hand as she moved past him. *Did she shudder?* They turned down a hall, passed partially opened doors, and stepped into a room at the end. A converted garage. Like the rest of the house, not a job well done.

Raw OSB board had been nailed over the roll-up door opening. The walls were unfinished leaving the studs exposed. The space had no windows. Several tall lamps stood around the cold room, some leaned precariously, but they all shone weak light on the chunks of a few mismatched pieces of carpet on the oil stained cement. Ammanda and Emmilie stood between the pool and ping pong tables and talked with a small group of girls and boys their age.

Molly continued to the far back corner where a seventies style bar with leather trim sat in front of glass shelves laden with liquor bottles. "What's your pleasure today? Moscow Mule, Whiskey Sour, or straight whiskey?"

Jeff had stopped in the middle of the make-shift game room the minute he'd spotted the alcohol. His heart pounded and throbbed in his ears. While heat flooded his body and formed sweat, his skin chilled. His stomach rolled like he stood on a ship tossed by a fierce storm. He closed his eyes and tried to breathe in deep and slow and hoped the nausea would pass. It didn't. *I need to get out. I don't belong here.*

"Tate? What are you drinking?"

She wouldn't call him by his first name. She'd abandoned his last name and tried to erase it from his daughters—though it had never legally been changed. Ammanda had said something about the price of changing a name being too expensive for Molly to manage for both girls and herself.

"I don't drink."

"Oh, you won't be driving again for hours, one drink isn't gonna …"

"I haven't had a drink since that night." Jeff turned on his heel. He was going to be sick. The doorbell rang at the other end of the oddly configured house. "I'll get it."

As Jeff staggered down the hall, he noticed a wire wastebasket in one of the rooms. The box he'd spent years lovingly filling with words of love for Emmilie sat tipped into it. Tattered envelopes were scattered, emptied of their cards and devoid of the money inside. His notes and messages to her were left unopened.

This had to be his second biggest mistake of his entire life. He fought tears as he made it to the front door and jerked it open. As he held it and stood there, Jeff noted the ratty and torn furniture in the living room.

"Yo. Em-Mers, what's up? Oh, hey dude …" The boy in his mid-twenties, hair in his face and jeans sagging stared at him confused.

"They're in the—"

"Par-Tayy room," the boy sang as he walked past Jeff and yelled down the hall. "Em-Mers girl, where you at?"

Gray clouds swirled outside as Jeff gripped the weathered door by its tarnished knob.

"You aren't running away again are you?" Molly stood with fists on her hips at the opening of the hall.

Chapter 54

Jessica glanced at the time again and sighed. Licorice perked up her ears and looked at her. "Jeff should be there by now. Thought he might call on his way." The little black dog tipped her head. "I'm sure he's fine, but he's grown quiet since he met Ammanda."

Licorice snuggled down again and closed her eyes, not at all interested in her human's ramblings.

Lord, be with Jeff today. Help him reconnect with his daughters. Make their time sweet. She struggled to come up with words for what she hoped would happen with the ex. She wanted them to get along for the girls' sake, but … what if he decided to get back with her? What if he moved to be closer to his daughters? He had the right to be a part of their lives. They'd missed so much time together. Their relationship deserved a chance to grow. What verse talked about God restoring what the locust took? Oh, she needed to memorize more.

Her hands sat still over her keyboard and her screen dimmed as her mind wandered. Jessica's thumb hit the trackpad, and the screen came back to life. "If only I could reset life as ease."

She'd broken her one rule. She let herself hope about the future. The more time she spent with Jeff, the easier it was for her to see the unimaginable possibility of being his wife. She'd waited for too long for this dream. How many memes had she seen about holding out for the *right* man? Hadn't thirty years been long enough? Abraham waited for twenty-five for the son God had promised, but he'd been married the entire time. Others in the Bible waited as well. Why did her delay seem unbearably long and utterly impossible? But it could all end this weekend. Jeff had already stopped talking to her about Ammanda's texts after the first few he'd received.

Ammanda's determination to get her parents back together had started to come between them. Didn't kids grow out of those childish dreams at some point? What if Jeff and Jessica had been married when Ammanda had met her dad?

Well, it would have made their current situation a lot easier now. There you go hoping again.

Jessica sighed and looked at her computer screen. Black again. She needed to get this website done in a couple of days. The business prepared for a rollout of a new product and needed the site ready to accept online orders prior to release date—no bugs—no glitches.

"Get back to it, Jessica, or you're going to lose this commission and it will tarnish your reputation before you can get off the ground." Toffee poked her nose out from beneath the blanket she'd burrowed under. "Go back to sleep. I'm talking to myself again."

Jessica stared at her screen. The order page had an issue. The product images all needed to be the same size though the various items for sale were not. Why weren't the pieces fitting together? Too much like her life at the moment. She sighed again and drew both dog's attention.

Jeff's grip on the still-open door turned his fingers white as his head snapped around to glare at Molly. "Run away! *You* are the one who ran off, took *my* children, and hid them for eighteen years. How can you accuse me of running anywhere?"

"Oh, come now," Molly sauntered the rest of the way into the room, sat on the couch, and patted the seat next to her. "What did you expect me to do? Let the girls suffer the shame and disgrace of having their father in jail?"

"But I didn't run away."

"Come, sit here and let's talk about this like adults. I'll refresh your memory." Her sickly-sweet smile turned his stomach. And her patronizing tone made Jeff want to throw something.

He didn't want to talk, and he definitely had no intention of sitting next to her. But he couldn't bring himself to leave and let her think he'd "run away" again.

"Emmie," a young woman dressed in a scandalously skimpy outfit bounced through the door. Her attire was unfit for the March day of barely over sixty degrees. In truth, what little she wore wouldn't be enough for a one hundred- and twenty-degree Arizona heat wave.

Jeff glanced away only to catch Molly smirking at him.

"Hey, Mrs. B." Two males followed the inappropriately dressed woman.

"Hey, all. Everyone's in the back. Grab a drink from the bar and enjoy," Molly said as Jeff glanced outside for anyone else before he closed the door.

He plopped in a chair on the opposite side of the coffee table from her and regretted it immediately as a spring poked him in the rump. Stale dusty air filled the room from his action.

Molly chuckled at him. "I don't remember you being such a prude."

"I'm not the man you left eighteen years ago."

She flipped her hand through the air as if brushing aside his statement like a gnat. "Don't go blaming me. You ran out that night. I tried to have a reasonable conversation with you about the girls' dance classes and—"

It all flooded back.

Chapter 55

Jeff's mind whirled back to the events of that horrible night. One comment from his ex-wife and it hit him like a raging horse. The argument that triggered him to leave the house, go to the bar, drink too much, and try to drive home screamed in this brain. Molly had enrolled both girls in dance as well as signing Ammanda in gymnastics and Emmilie in some pageant—at eight. Jeff worked fifty hours a week but failed to keep up with Molly's spending. The classes were far beyond his budget. But she refused to get a job herself to help with the cost of all the activities she wanted the girls involved in or for any of her shopping. Jeff could never meet all of her demands.

Molly continued to drone on about his shortcomings. "I tried hard to keep it all together, and you fought me at every turn. You couldn't see how much these opportunities would have benefited your daughters."

Jeff leaned his forearms on his thighs and made sure to cause his right sleeve to slide up and expose more of his scars. He stared at her eyes. "Did you enroll them after you left me?"

"How could I without you paying your fair share?"

"I would have paid—had you'd shared where you'd hidden away my girls. Seems like they survived without all those classes."

Her hand flipped back and forth in the air again, like a salmon swimming upstream. "Enough of this talk of the past. There is no going back and undoing what you did then." Her gaze flitted to his scars now and then but never lingered.

Emmilie nearly skipped into the room. "Hey, I need $120."

Jeff turned and saw she'd spoken to him. "What?"

"I heard Venom's Curse is performing at the Selland. I have to go."

Jeff stared at her. "What about the money from your box?" There had to be at least $200 he'd saved for her through the years.

She waved her hand over her tattered jeans and garish blouse with her belly exposed. "You don't expect me to go around in last year's styles, do you? I had to go shopping as soon as Mandie told me about the box of money."

"You already spent all your money before you even got it—on a new wardrobe?" Jeff struggled not to raise his voice.

Emmilie laughed. "Don't be silly. The little bit of cash only got me a new pair of shoes, a pair of jeans and two tops."

Her extravagant spending made his head throb. "I don't carry wads of cash on me," Jeff hoped his lack of immediate funds would put an end to this discussion.

Emmilie held out her hand. "It's okay, it's easier if I use your credit card."

"I don't use one other than for emergencies and I don't carry it on me." He didn't lie to her outright, but he didn't speak the full truth either. He rarely used his card, but he did have one—in his wallet he'd locked in his glove box.

Emmilie shrugged and turned back down the hall. "You can text me the number later. But I'll need it by tomorrow to get good seats."

Jeff stared after her.

"You have funds." Molly glared at him with a slow shake of her head. "That computer business of yours helps companies get secure networks. It brings in money. Surely, a concert ticket wouldn't put you out."

"I'm not a bank. I watch every dollar, because I have business expenses, especially with the horses."

Molly wrinkled her nose. "Think of all the money you'll save and how much the girls will love you for the treasures you'll buy them once you move down here and get rid of those filthy animals.”

“Who said I wanted to move here? I have a life in Elk Grove. I’m very happy there, and I love the work I do rehabilitating the horses to give them to the center where they can be with people who really need them. It’s important work.”

“But what about your daughters? Don’t you care about them?”

“Of course, I do. I love them. I’ll still love them the same from Elk Grove and continue to do the work I enjoy. It keeps me fit and financially stable to meet my needs. But I’m not rich.”

“How can you say you love them if you won’t even get Emmilie a single concert ticket?”

“I can see your attitudes haven’t changed much, Molly. Buying *things* is not love. I know what real love is. It has nothing to do with a single cent.”

“But it shows how you feel—”

“No, I’ve experienced true love.”

“From the girl you’re seeing?” Molly’s face scrunched up as though she’d eaten expired meat.

“Yes, Jessica introduced me to God. I’m a Christian now.”

Molly’s mouth started to drop, but she recovered quickly. “Oh, isn’t that nice.” She looked at him for a moment. “You know the good book says God hates divorce. I guess I don’t even need to ask you—now—after all you’re a Bible thumper—but when will you move home?”

“This isn’t my home.”

“But the girls’ lives are here. It is the only logical solution. You’ll move here and everything will be fine again.”

Chapter 56

Jeff's heart pounded out a wild beat like a maraca shaken by a crazed ape. He couldn't breathe.

The alarm on his phone went off in his pocket. Jeff had no idea why. *Thank you, Lord.* He pushed to his feet and stood on wobbly legs as the clanging from his hip continued to fill the air. "I've got to head out." To *my* home. Where I intend to live for a good long time. I'm never … The thought faded like a visible breath on a cold day. If his girls were here, he'd no doubt be back.

Molly rested into the couch and leaned her head against her fist. "Well, it's been a brief visit." She sighed. "I'm sure you'll make it up to the girls when you move in. I'll set up an air mattress for you in the play room—unless you intend to move back in fully." One eyebrow rose. "Tomorrow, I'll start looking for a new place for us."

"No!" Jeff tried not to scream as he finally silenced the alarm. He pushed up his sleeves and watched Molly's reaction. Her gaze slid to his scarred arm. Her eyes closed as a faint shudder rattled through her. It could never work. He would never get back together with this woman. "I haven't agreed to anything."

Molly shrugged. "You will, if you take this religion thing seriously."

Jeff staggered outside and across the street to his truck. He jerked open the door.

"Dad," Ammanda bounded toward him. "You aren't leaving already, are you?"

"Need to get home," Jeff could barely form words.

"But you and Mom talked, right? We're going to be a family again, aren't we, Daddy?"

Jeff leaned against the side of his truck. "Ammanda, I don't know. I'm not the same man your mother abandoned all those years ago. My situation is different now. I've made a great life for myself." He wanted to tell his daughter no, he'd never get back with her mother, but he couldn't hurt Ammanda. Molly's comment about God hating divorce nagged at him almost as much as she did.

Ammanda looped her arm in his. "But Daddy, I want you in my life again."

"I know, and I want you in my life too. But Ammanda, having me in your life may not mean getting back with your mother. Our relationships look different now. You're all grown up and you won't be living at home much longer."

She laid her head on his shoulder. "*Please*, Daddy."

"Give me some time." Jeff pulled away from her and stepped into his truck's cab. He closed the door, turned over the engine, and tried not to gun it down the street. He looked in his rear-view mirror. Ammanda remained standing in the middle of the road. He couldn't get away fast enough.

Jessica had finally gotten the sales page of the website to look like she wanted, but for some reason her stomach rolled, and she thought she might be sick. She couldn't throw up on her new computer. She set it aside and moved to lie on the couch for a moment. Licorice and Toffee jumped on her as if she'd changed location to play with them. She stood and stepped to the sliding glass door to let them out. She panted for breath as if she trudged up a mountain side. *What is the matter with me?*

Jeff. There'd been no message from him all day. She didn't *know* anything troubled him. But something *felt* very wrong.

Her girls demanded to be let in. Licorice sprang against the glass door to make the urgency of her request known.

Jess turned away from the door and walked across the living room toward the hall. Her stomach heaved. She didn't make it to the bathroom before her knees gave out and she dropped to the carpet.

Jeff. He was the one thought that filled her mind.

"Lord, I don't know what's going on, but Jeff needs You right now. Be at his side. Cover him with Your mighty hands and hold him tight."

Air filled her lungs and the nausea left. She rested back on her rump and leaned against the wall. Nothing like that had ever happened to her before. Her head relaxed and touched the textured plaster. "Lord, cradle Jeff in Your loving arms." Her prayer came much calmer now. "He needs to feel Your presence. Grant him Your wisdom and let him see the situation and his family with Your eyes. Let Your love and peace fill him and erase all doubt."

Chapter 57

Jeff sped onto Highway 99 and wove around traffic as his speed reached upwards of eighty miles an hour. "I can't go back." He yelled at the windshield. "No way am I ever living with *that* woman again. Not in a filthy house filled with booze. I can't. I *won't* go back to my old life."

Cars whizzed past in a blur of color. He slammed on the brakes to avoid hitting one car, jerked into the next lane and cut someone else off. Horns blared, but he ignored them. He had to get away.

She is still disgusted by my scars. How can I live with a woman who is repulsed when she looks at me? What about Jess? I love her. I hate Molly. Jeff gulped. He knew he shouldn't hate *anyone*—but his emotions were in control at the moment.

He came up too fast on another car with nowhere to go. A momentary flash back to the last time he'd hit a car seized his heart. He jerked the wheel to the right, careened for the ditch alongside the road, swerved back into traffic, and ended up on the shoulder. But he kept driving. Gravel kicked up from his tires, and he fish-tailed for several hundred feet. At last, he slowed to a more manageable speed—though still over the limit—and re-entered the lanes of traffic.

"What am I supposed to do? Molly wants a better house. Emmilie only wants what I can buy her. I can't live with their greed and materialism and I *can't* forgive Molly for all she's done."

It felt as though something slammed into Jeff's chest and drove out his breath. He swerved onto a narrow dirt road off the highway and skidded to a stop in a cloud of dust. Newly plowed fields sat on either side of him. He gulped air. He'd been forgiven everything. Restored completely and welcomed into the family he'd injured with such love it brought fresh tears to his eyes.

"Is this why I'm here, God? I have to forgive Molly like I have been forgiven? I have to accept this responsibility and restore her like You did me?"

He gripped the steering wheel hard enough his hands went numb. Forgive her and mend their relationship. Could he go through with it? What about Jess? What about his happy life? Could God ask him to throw all of it away? But he knew the freedom and soul-changing power of forgiveness. It had driven him into the Lord's arms. Molly needed God too. As did his girls. Could God make their salvation story happen by sending him back to restore his old family?

He clung to the steering wheel as his thought wrestled with God. He glanced at the dashboard clock. Had he sat here beside the freeway for over a half an hour? Finally, Jeff released the breath held in his lungs. "All right, Lord. If it's Your will for me to get back with Molly, then I will do it. To tell the truth, I hope it isn't the case, but I will be obedient."

Jeff's gaze caught on a church bulletin on the seat beside him. He stretched and wiggled his fingers to get the blood flowing again, then picked it up. He flipped it to the back where it had the contact information listed and pulled his phone from his pocket. The church answering machine responded. He waited for the beep. "I know the office is closed but, Pastor Matt I need to talk with you ASAP. It's urgent. Please, as soon as you can, I need to meet with you."

Jeff pressed END, took a deep breath, turned his truck around, and got back on the freeway. He drove the speed limit this time. He kept repeating, "I'll do what God wants. I *will* do what God wants."

Jeff pulled into the church parking lot after 8 p.m. Pastor Matt stood at the office door and waited for Jeff to join him. "Thank you for meeting with me. I know it's late and you have to preach in the morning.

I really need this."

Pastor Matt patted him on the shoulder. "Come into my office." They sat opposite the small desk and Pastor smiled at him. "We better start with prayer."

"Definitely. Make it good." Though Jeff bowed his head, his mind rambled with warring thoughts. He caught the gist. Pastor asked for the Lord to give Jeff the answers he needed. Yep, he'd said the right prayer.

Jeff spent the next hour telling the pastor his life story. Married right out of high school, the challenges of his marriage, the ungodly lifestyle, drinking, the accident, and jail. Then fast-forward to nine months ago and the wonder of Jess. Her acceptance of him—scars and all—meeting the Morgan's and their utter forgiveness of him, Jeff giving his life to Christ, and most recently connecting with his girls, which brought the story to his time with Molly today.

"Pastor Matt, I can't believe I'm back here in this place with my ex again. We never should have married in the first place and now she expects to get back together as though she never abandoned me and stole my kids." Jeff finally took a breath. If Pastor had wanted to say anything, Jeff had never given him a second to get a word in. "But I also know forgiveness. It's … It's …"

"Amazing," Pastor offered.

"Yeah, like amazing squared. I know Molly, Emmilie, and Ammanda need the Lord. I love Jess and to go back to Molly would break Jess' heart—it would break mine too. But I know I need to take my relationship with God seriously and no one can come before Him. If God wants me to remarry Molly, I will." Jeff slid back in his chair and stared at Pastor Matt. "Is re-marrying Molly what I need to do?"

Pastor now moved to the edge of his seat. His forearms rested on his desk, and he opened his Bible. His face filled with a huge smile. "Let me tell you what God's says about this very issue."

Chapter 58

It seemed like an eternity since Jessica sat alone in church. It hadn't been. Jeff entered her life less than a year ago. But in their time together, she'd come to the point where she didn't recognize herself anymore. She'd quit her job, started her own company, and—though it was terrifying, she had to admit—she'd fallen in love.

But Jeff didn't sit beside her today. He might not ever again. Jessica had gotten a cryptic text from him late last night.

"So much to tell you. Won't be at church tomorrow. Have to deal with some stuff. Talk soon."

What did he mean? Deal with what stuff? Had his girls convinced him to get back with his ex? The nausea from yesterday evening returned. Unshed tears burned. Why had she ever let herself hope?

Pastor Matt spoke about the way God moved and how the road may seem twisty with hair-pin turns, steep grades, and sheer cliffs at the edge.

"But the truth is, our loving Father has gone before us, paved the way smooth, installed guardrails to protect us, and assures our route will take us to the beautiful place He always intended for us to be."

Did he look at her with a smile when he said those words? Tears filled her lids, blurred her vision, and made her see things that weren't there. Pastor Matt gazed out over the entire congregation and didn't direct his comments at her. Right? When the inevitable happened, and Jeff told her he would be going back to his family, she would never recover.

Sunday *and* Monday passed with no word from Jeff. In the last few months he barely made it a handful of hours without at least a text. But now—nothing. Bone-crushing, spirit-shattering, silence.

Tuesday afternoon and she still hadn't heard anything. Doubt assailed her. She knew she'd never hear from him again. She should call and get some answers. In truth, she didn't want to listen to what he had to tell her. Jessica did what she always did. She ignored the irrational shattering of her heart and threw herself into her work. She skipped meals, got up in the middle of the night because she couldn't sleep, completed two websites and had made good headway on another.

Licorice jumped on the recliner where she did most of her work, walked up her legs, and pushed her laptop closed. Her ears perked up and her tail wagged excitedly. "Well, at least someone is still hungry."

Jessica set the laptop aside and stood. The dogs ran to the kitchen. When had she last eaten? Probably not a good thing if she couldn't remember. The thought of food made her stomach knot, but she should try to—

Her phone whistled.

Her heart fell clear to her toes.

Did she read it?

What if a client needed her?

What if it wasn't?

What if Jeff tried to reach her?

How had she fallen into this self-doubt, pessimistic gloom this quickly? Her life had been good. Her emotions weren't dragging her down. She rubbed at the old cuts on the thigh. They itched.

Jeff. It always came back to him. He strengthened her. Made her believe in herself.

Jessica sighed as the girls ran back into the living room to see if she still intended to feed them. "I am a child of God. I shouldn't need a man to complete me." She didn't even convince herself. Why couldn't she believe what God said about her and stand in His strength regardless of what Jeff did or didn't do? When would she break out of this emotional whiplash?

She closed her eyes and tried to get a grip on her flailing insecurities. They were like a hose turned up too high, spraying anxiety and drenching every part of her with dread. *The worst thing he can say is he'll never see me again—and I already know it.*

She picked up the phone and swiped it on.

A message from Jeff glared back at her. "Meet me at the park."

She couldn't decide if she appreciated a man who wouldn't break off their relationship over a text. She'd never been one to rip off a band-aid. She'd work at it for an hour if need be to save herself any pain. Still, she'd ended up being a cutter. In the end, procrastination didn't work—it prolonged the hurt. She rubbed her leg again.

Jessica still held the phone trying to decide if she should answer, and if she did what she'd say, when another text popped up.

"Are you coming?"

Show some guts, woman. What happened to 'Be bold?' Yeah, that had served her well. Fine. Let's get this over with.

"Yes," she texted back with a heavy sigh.

She left the girls at home and walked down the street toward the park. It had been good while it lasted. She at least had the memories of dating *someone*. She and God had managed before. Jessica scratched at her scars. Surely, she'd find a way to be content again. "He will never leave you nor forsake you," she repeated as she walked. Too bad the *he* in her wishful thoughts didn't completely refer to the Lord.

Chapter 59

Jeff sat at the far side of the table they often frequented. His arms rested on the top. He stayed seated as she approached. "I didn't think you'd ever get here."

Did he sound annoyed with her? Excited? She couldn't read his expression—or maybe she didn't want to.

A group gathered at another table over the rise to her right. It wasn't good picnic weather, but her chill could be coming from more than the spring breeze. She forgot about the others and slid onto the bench opposite Jeff.

"I have a lot to tell you," he started.

Jessica wanted him to get it over with. She didn't need all the messy details. But he seemed intent on telling about his time with Emmilie, Ammanda, and Molly. And he talked at hyper speed.

"Emmilie took my box, emptied it of all the cash, and tossed the rest. Molly kept saying how we were going to get back together. She asked when I would be moving *home* with them. After a long fight with God, I told Him I'd do it if He wanted me to."

Tears filled Jessica's eyes. She knew her heart cracked.

"I drove away like the devil himself pursued me—and in a way, he might have been. It's a miracle I didn't get a ticket or hit someone."

"When did that happen?"

Jeff paused to think. "I guess about 5 p.m. Saturday 'cause I didn't get to the church until about 8 p.m. Pastor Matt graciously met with me at that hour."

He'd been careening down the freeway at the same time Jessica had felt sick and ended up on her knees in prayer. What a strange coincidence.

"Anyway, I told Pastor Matt my whole story—my entire life." Now Jeff's smile grew. "This is what he told me. Molly is not a believer. She still has alcohol in her home. But what's most important is God says in Deuteronomy, a person cannot remarry a former spouse if one of them has been married since the divorce. Molly has been married four times since she left me and lived with a few others. There is no going back."

What did that mean? He would break up with Jessica but *not* remarry Molly? Why did it sound like he spoke from under water? Did the group from the other picnic table move closer?

"Sunday, I went back down to Fresno and met Molly in a park near her home. I told her I could not do what she asked. I forgave her, and I told her I would help the girls where I could, but I would not be in their lives the way she wanted. She was furious …"

The other group definitely approached them. Jeff continued to meander around his point.

Jessica looked more closely at the strangers. But they were people she knew. Her parents were there. Pastor Matt, David, the Hansens. The ending of her relationship with Jeff had caused a mental break down.

Jessica turned to look back at Jeff, but he wasn't on the bench. He knelt beside her on one knee, and he held a small jewelry box.

"Jessica Ann Easton, I have been in love with you almost since the first day we met. I know it's only been a few months, but I know I want to spend the rest of my life with you and no one else. God has completely changed my life, and He used you to make the change happen. I can't wait another moment to ask you to be my wife."

Jessica stared at him. Somewhere in her befuddled brain she registered his words. Tears slid down her cheeks in endless streams.

Jeff's brow rose. "Is that a yes?"

His whole talk hadn't been about an ending but a beginning. She had every reason to hope. She'd been petulant, impatient, and whiny, but God—as always—had been faithful, loving, and kind. This man, the one kneeling here with an engagement ring, had turned out to be more than she could have ever imagined or asked for.

At last, Jessica shook off her stupor, nodded her head, and threw her arms around his neck.

He hugged her with a bear-like grip and whispered in her ear. "You thought I called you here to break up with you, didn't you?"

"Yes."

He pulled from her enough to see her face. "You're stuck with me. I'll never let you go." His lips pressed to hers, and the small park filled with cheers.

About the Author

Michelle Janene (Murray) works part-time in her church's office by day
and writes in a wide rage of genres in all her free time.
She lives in Northern California with two crazy dogs and the characters of her imagination.

If you enjoyed *Found in the Scars* please review it on your favorite site.

Join Michelle's email list and get a free novelette at
MichelleJanene.com
You can also connect with Michelle on:
Facebook: Michelle Janene-Author or Strong Tower Press
Twitter: @MichelleJaneneM
Instagram: michellejanene_author
Pinterest: www.pinterest.com/michellejanene
Goodreads: Michelle Janene
StrongTowerPress.com

Other Books

Check out these books also by Michelle

Mission: Mistaken Identity

The Changed Heart Series:
God's Rebel
Rebel's Son
Hidden Rebel

Seer of Windmere

Barbarian Hero

Guardians of Truth

Culling a Miracle

Savior Stones Chronicles
Lost Stones